Showdown in Durango

"You there," Slocum called.

Nestor turned and saw the silhouette of a tall man framed in the light from the open door behind him. He wheeled and his hand darted downward for his pistol.

"Back off!" Nestor yelled as his hand pulled his pistol from its holster.

Slocum crouched and his hand was like lightning as it streaked for his .45 Colt. Before Nestor's gun could clear leather, Slocum's pistol was hip-high in his hand and his thumb pressed down on the hammer to cock it.

There was a loud click in the empty storage building and Nestor knew he had a split second to live.

"Damn you," he growled.

Slocum's finger squeezed the trigger and his pistol roared.

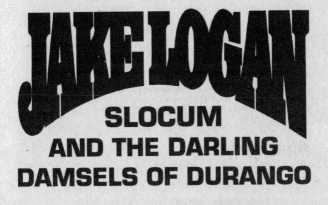

JAKE LOGAN

SLOCUM
AND THE DARLING
DAMSELS OF DURANGO

DISCARD

JOVE BOOKS, NEW YORK

THE BERKLEY PUBLISHING GROUP
Published by the Penguin Group
Penguin Group (USA) LLC
375 Hudson Street, New York, New York 10014

USA • Canada • UK • Ireland • Australia • New Zealand • India • South Africa • China

penguin.com

A Penguin Random House Company

SLOCUM AND THE DARLING DAMSELS OF DURANGO

A Jove Book / published by arrangement with the author

For information, address: The Berkley Publishing Group,
a division of Penguin Group (USA) LLC,
375 Hudson Street, New York, New York 10014.

ISBN: 978-0-515-15436-8

PUBLISHING HISTORY
Jove mass-market edition / January 2014

PRINTED IN THE UNITED STATES OF AMERICA

10 9 8 7 6 5 4 3 2 1

Cover illustration by Sergio Giovine.

1

John Slocum jerked hard on the reins as an explosion erupted from a black hole in the side of the mountain. Stones and dust blew from the mine shaft. He and his horse, Ferro, were showered with splinters of wood and sand. The other horses on his string all backed down on their haunches as the concussion shattered their senses.

A body sailed from the cave. Lifeless and bloody, the corpse shot sixty feet down the mountainside. It tumbled over and over like an oversized rag doll. It bounced off rocks, leaving spatters of blood like some nightmarish stain everywhere it landed and bounced.

Finally, the body came to rest at the bottom of a narrow canyon. Above the smoky mine, Slocum saw a figure stand up and stare down at the broken body below.

Man or woman?

Slocum couldn't tell. The figure wore a slouch hat, a man's plaid shirt, bib overalls, and work boots. Unarmed. A black detonator box with the plunger down stood at the feet of the figure.

Ferro fought the bit and cranked his head as he fishtailed off the narrow trail and shot out his forelegs to stop himself before plunging down in the canyon.

The figure on the rimrock heard the noise and stared at the man in black clothing on a black horse with a string of four other horses on a rope he held in his left hand.

Slocum caught a glimpse of the face. Small, oval-shaped. Long strands of straw blond hair streamed from under the shapeless slouch hat.

Then, the figure turned and ran into the timber.

Small feet, small frame, thin and shapely arms, hips that were rounded, curved like a woman's. A grown woman's.

It didn't make sense.

Slocum saw the wires dangling down from the detonator, dangling over the mine entrance with their bitter ends swaying back and forth, in and out, of the smoking hole in the mountain.

Deliberate, Slocum thought. He knew.

Whoever had pushed down on that plunger knew that there were wires connected to sticks of dynamite.

Murder. Cold-blooded murder.

He heard voices. Female voices. Brief and unintelligible. Breathless. A few seconds later, he heard a thrashing of leaves and hoofbeats that faded into silence.

Slocum stepped out of the saddle, tied the lead rope to a small pine tree off the side of the Old Spanish Trail, then ground-tied Ferro to a small bush on the canyon side. He walked a zigzag course down the slope, the heels of his black stovepipe boots bracing him. He wore spurs without rowels, and these served as a safety measure when a heel slipped on soft dirt.

A lone hawk dragged its shadow over the ground as Slocum hunkered down to see if there was any chance the man blown from the mine was still alive.

He touched two fingers to the man's neck, just under the ear, and felt for a pulse.

There was none.

The man wore a checkered cotton shirt, a bandanna around his neck, brownish wool trousers, and work boots. The back of his shirt was blackened with soot and there was a hole in the back of his head with a long sliver of bloody wood jutting from it. He appeared to be in his late twenties or early thirties. His hands were calloused and grimy, dirt under the fingernails. He hadn't shaved in at least three days, there were tobacco stains on his lips, and his teeth were caked with chewing tobacco.

Slocum wondered if he had been the only one working the mine. When he looked up, he saw the tail end of an ore car on rails.

Most of the smoke had blown away, but the entrance to the mine still danced with dust motes that were caught in the sun's rays like ghostly fireflies.

It was a steep climb up to the mine over slippery talus tailings, but Slocum managed by pulling on the branches of small bushes and a boulder or two that were buried in earth.

He stood up in front of the mine and listened.

The mine was as silent as a tomb.

"Hello," he called. "Anybody in there?"

His voice sounded hollow as it bounced off the walls and wooden shoring. The frame just inside the adit was splintered and pocked from the blast. It was a large mine, but he would have to duck some if he entered.

He called out again.

No one answered.

And he heard no signs of life from inside.

He slid and staggered down the slope from the ledge in front of the mine. He had to dig in his heels and grab at bushes to keep from pitching forward onto his face.

As he stepped past the dead man, he thought that someone in town might come out and retrieve the body. He did not fancy carrying it up the slope to where Ferro was tethered.

Durango was not far by his reckoning.

It wasn't really a town yet, but that was what people were calling it. Durango. He had learned that there was a city in Spain by that name, and it came from a Basque word "Urango," which meant something like "a messy place." And it was messy, with its clapboard dwellings and buildings, messy with prospectors and gold miners, merchants, cardsharps, whores, gamblers, hardware drummers, and the like. It was dusty and thriving, with the Rio de Las Animas running right through it, its waters laden with dust and silt, murky as a shadow until it flowed past the settlement.

He had horses to deliver to a freight hauler he had met in Pueblo, Lou Darvin, who had worn out two teams in the little boomtown in the heart of the Rocky Mountains. The Animas

Freight Company was a booming business for Darvin, who hauled in goods from Trinity and as far away as Denver. He paid top dollar for good horses, and Slocum had four of them he had brought down from Cheyenne and Denver. He had leased a corral in the Denver stockyards and had a remuda waiting there in case anyone else in town wanted to buy from him.

He untied the horses on the lead rope and walked to Ferro. His tall gelding, sixteen hands high, pawed the ground and swished his tail. When Slocum untied him, he tossed his black mane and snorted through wet rubbery nostrils.

"Easy, boy," Slocum said as he set his foot in the stirrup and hauled himself into the saddle by holding on to the saddle horn.

In moments he was back on the wide Spanish Trail, which coursed through a canyon with steep walls, rocky crags, and jutting boulders. The air was thin and fresh, with the scent of fir and spruce, the cheep of chipmunks as they scampered over and behind rocks or dove into small holes as he passed.

He began to see wagons and men on the bare backs of mules as he reached the edge of town. And he heard the din of commerce amid the dust and the burbling of the Animas River, which he crossed on a sturdy wooden bridge. He turned left and rode toward Main Street, which teemed with men and women going in and out of stores or walking along, carrying picks, shovels, axes, and the ever-present pans they used to sift gold from the sands of the river.

Darvin's freight company was well down Main, and Slocum headed there as passersby gawked at the tall man on the black horse, dressed in black himself from the crown of his Stetson to the soles of his stovepipe boots. Some waved, some admired the horses, and others dashed out of his path. He rode by the constable's small office and the jail next to it, the Mother Lode Saloon and Art's Card House next to it, Barry's Mercantile, Logan Investments, and the Rio Grande Dry Goods Store. Mexicans hawked blankets and clay bowls, turquoise jewelry and knives with ornate brass handles, trinkets for women and kids, their wares on tables outside *tiendas* and restaurants. There was Molly's Café with its sign promising GOOD EATS and another small Mexican cantina, El Rincón, at the end of one block. He passed Julie's Boardinghouse. On the second-floor balcony sat three pretty young women in skimpy skirts and revealing blouses. They all waved at Slocum, and he waved back at their becoming smiles.

Slocum reined Ferro to a halt in front of the freight company. There was a hitch rail more than twenty feet long, a loading dock in front of the entrance. He tied the small remuda to the post of the hitch rail after he wrapped Ferro's reins around the top rail.

The sign over the establishment proclaimed it to be the ANIMAS FREIGHT COMPANY. Underneath were the words PROPRIETOR, LOUIS DARVIN.

The horses Slocum had on the rope whinnied when he dismounted.

Lou Darvin emerged from the building and stood spread-legged on the loading platform.

"Good-lookin' string you got there, Slocum," he said. Darvin was a five-foot-ten-inch block of a man with a vat of a chest, bright hazel eyes, and a face that looked as if it had been carved out of a solid chunk of hickory, with high cheekbones, a bulb of a nose, and a chin that sported a small goatee. He looked like a lumberjack, which was what he had once been before he came to Durango and opened up his hauling business.

"They'll do you, Lou," Slocum said, "if you take good care of them."

"Haw. It's the mountains that gets 'em, not hauling my wagons."

"The mountains get everything in the end," Slocum said as he climbed the stairs.

He and Darvin shook hands.

"Come on into the office and I'll pay you the balance on those horses," Lou said.

"Want me to put them up in your barn out back?" Slocum asked.

"Naw. Jasper will take care of them."

They entered the warehouse and Lou called out to Jasper Nichols, who was setting wooden boxes on shelves for shipment.

"Comin'," Jasper said as he shoved a box onto a shelf next to several others.

"Got some horses out front, Jasper," Darvin told the young man, a slender lad with blond peach fuzz on his cheeks and chin, lean and supple, with hard muscles in his arms from lifting and handling freight. He wore denim trousers and a checkered shirt, a match to the one Slocum had seen on the dead man back up in the canyon.

"I'll take care of 'em, Lou," Nichols said and flashed a gaptoothed smile as he passed the two men in front of Lou's office.

"He's a good boy," Lou said as they entered his office. "Still a little wet behind the ears, but a quick learner."

"Is there a sale on those checked shirts?" Slocum asked as Lou walked around his desk and Slocum sat in a round-backed wooden chair.

"Huh?" Lou asked as he sat down and pulled out a drawer, lifted a cash box onto his desk.

"I saw that same kind of shirt on a man who just got blown out of a mine outside of town."

"What?"

"Someone set off a charge of dynamite inside a mine and this feller blew out. Killed him."

"Where was this mine exactly?" Lou asked. He took a key from his pocket and unlocked the cash box.

Slocum told him.

"Damn," Lou said. "Jasper's brother had him a mine there. Older brother. His name was Wilbur Nichols. Dead you say?"

"Deliberately. I saw someone up on the rimrock blow the dynamite and run off into the timber."

"The hell you say. Get a good look at the man?"

Slocum stretched his legs out and leaned back in the chair.

"It wasn't a man," Slocum said. "It was a woman, I think. And there were at least two of them. They rode off through the timber."

"A woman?" Lou said as he picked up a sheaf of stacked bills from the cash box.

"A woman, Lou. Maybe a scorned one."

"A scorned one?"

"Hell hath no fury . . ." Slocum said.

Lou blanched as color drained from his cheeks. He swallowed hard and closed his eyes.

"Like a woman scorned," Lou murmured, finishing the sentence.

Outside, the horses whickered as Jasper led them around back to the barn and corral.

A shaft of sunlight streamed through the pane of the office window. Dust motes danced in the beam like tiny insects flashing gold in imitation of fireflies.

2

Lou counted out several bills and handed them across the desk to Slocum. The color returned to his cheeks, but now he had a steely glint in his eyes as he looked at Slocum.

"You tell anybody about this, Slocum?"

"I rode straight here. Man's down in a deep gulley and I didn't want to lug him up, tie him on one of the horses, and bring his body into town."

"You've got to tell the constable. Abner Hellinger. Abner ain't much, but he's all we got. He'll get some men to retrieve Wilbur's body. God, I hate to tell Jasper about this. He doted on his big brother."

"I'll take care of telling the constable. That was my next stop."

"I got a room for you at the hotel. Sometimes it gets pretty full. Just sign the register. I got the bill."

"Thanks, Lou. Buy you a drink later?"

"We'll probably close up early because Jasper's goin' to cave in on me. No shipments today. Not until tomorrow. Saloon okay with you?"

"I know where it is," Slocum said. "Any idea who might have pushed down on that plunger?"

"I know Wil had him a gal a month or so ago. They broke up, I heard."

"Know her?"

"Naw. I think her name was Silvia or Sybil. Somethin' like that. She was a hellion, Wil said. Went through men in town like shit through a tin horn."

Slocum stood up, brushed dust off his black trousers. Squared his hat.

"I'll see you at the saloon, Lou. Thanks for the cash."

"I knowed that was quite a trip across the mountains to get here. You had your hands full."

"What with rattlesnakes scaring the horses and bear scat on the road and cougars in the night screaming like banshees, yeah, it was quite a trip, Lou."

"Those horses will keep me in business for some time."

"Let me know when you want some more," Slocum said. He bowed his head slightly and touched a finger to the tip of his hat in farewell.

"See you at the saloon later," Lou said.

Slocum rode back up the street and stopped at the constable's office. He wrapped his reins around the hitch rail, patted Ferro on the neck, and went inside the small log building.

A short man with smoked eyeglasses looked up. He was trying to thread a needle. A gabardine vest sat on his desk with a loose button next to it.

"Mornin'," Abner Hellinger said as he looked up. "What's on your mind, stranger?"

"I want to report a dead man east of town."

"Well, set down and tell me about it," Abner said. He shoved the vest aside and slid a notepad in its place. He grabbed a pencil and adjusted his eyeglasses.

Slocum sat down in a round-backed chair with most of the paint worn off the back and the struts.

Slocum told him about the blast and the name Lou had given him. Abner jotted down certain items on the notepad.

"Hmm," the constable said. "Wilbur Nichols, eh? You say the killer was a woman?"

"Yes, from what little I saw of her, I'd say it was a woman. Maybe two."

"Two?"

"I heard another voice in the timber. It sounded female."

"That's mighty unusual," Abner said.

"Curious, I'd say," Slocum said.

"Yeah. Mighty curious. A female murderer. Don't get many of them in my line of work. We've had a few killings here, mostly knives and Messicans, a gunshot or two. But 'twixt two men usually, not wimmin."

"Women have been known to kill, too," Slocum said. "What's curious about it is that this woman knew about dynamite and used it to blow a man up in broad daylight."

"Yeah, that is mighty surprisin'," Abner said. "Ain't no women workin' any of the mines hereabouts, far as I know."

"This woman had a grudge," Slocum said.

Abner sat up and laid his pencil down. He looked at Slocum over the top rims of his eyeglasses.

"A grudge? What makes you think that? And say, what's your name anyway?"

"John Slocum. Takes a lot of know-how to plant sticks of dynamite, run the wires to them, and drop them into the mine, then send a jolt of electricity down those wires to explode a cap and set off the explosion."

"Yes, it does," Abner admitted. He looked away from Slocum for a minute and tapped his fingers on his notepad. The taps made a faint rustling sound as the paper crinkled slightly.

"Was Wilbur married?" Slocum asked.

"Nope. I was just thinkin'. Sometime back, rumor was that he got in a fight of some sort with a woman. Don't know who the woman was, nor if the rumor was true. Nobody came here and filed a complaint."

"Who might know about this?" Slocum asked.

"You some kind of detective?" Abner asked.

"No. Just a curious horse trader," Slocum replied.

"It was just saloon talk, Mr. Slocum. You know how the boys jabber when they're swiggin' down their whiskeys and beers."

"The town hall," Slocum said.

Abner smiled. His apple cheeks rose and fell with every facial movement.

"Like the potbellied stove in the mercantile store. Sometimes I think men are worse gossips than the wimmin."

Slocum chuckled. "But," he said, "somebody here in town knows something. Something they're keeping secret."

"That's likely, too," Abner said. "Miners and prospectors are a closed-mouth bunch. They don't talk about their finds or tell where they're lookin'. Something like this, they might not want to get out. Wilbur was one of 'em and he had more'n one fistfight since he'd been here."

"What about Jasper? His brother?"

"Oh, Jasper, he's the meek one. Idolizes, I mean idolized, his older brother. Never no trouble with him that I know of."

"Well, thanks, Constable," Slocum said. "I'll be in town awhile. Lou got me a room at the hotel. Lou Darvin, I mean."

"Stay out of trouble. And call me Abner."

"Abner it is," Slocum said. He stood up and then left the office.

Abner sat there for a moment, then got up and took his hat off the coat tree. He had a body to pick up and take to the undertaker.

He watched Slocum lead his horse up the street toward the hotel.

The man looked familiar. Not that he had seen him in person before, but he might have seen a drawing of him on a wanted flyer.

He'd look through the stacks when he finished taking care of Wilbur Nichols's body, and taking a look at that plunger up above the Nichols mine.

He walked toward the saloon, where he hoped to find some volunteers to ride with him up the canyon.

It was a hell of a way to start his day.

3

The girls were still on the balcony when Slocum walked by, leading Ferro. They smiled and giggled, then waved at him again. The two women on the front porch watched him, but did not smile or wave. One of them was very pretty and looked familiar. He felt her eyes on him as he walked past.

One thing was certain, he thought. If he ever saw her again, he would recognize her for sure.

She was the prettiest one in the bunch, with her delicate face, long amber tresses, and a velvet choker around her delicate neck. And her long stockings could not hide those Thoroughbred racehorse legs. Nor could her gingham dress conceal her curvaceous body. He could not detect the color of her eyes at that distance, but her lips were full and luscious under a faint tinge of red lipstick.

He almost saluted her as he passed by, but that was not his style.

Slocum had a policy.

Let the women come to him, he thought as he tied Ferro up at the hitch rail outside the hotel and walked into the lobby.

The desk clerk had him sign the register and handed him a key.

"Down the hall, last door on your left," the clerk said. "And my name is Harvey Lesser."

"Thanks," Slocum said.

He walked down the hall and stopped at the last door on his left. Number 6. The key worked, and he entered the room. He had two windows with plenty of light. One looked out the back onto an alley, and a fenced lot that was empty. The other gave him a view of the building next door, clapboard siding with fading brown paint. There was a bed, a wardrobe, a dresser, a table and two chairs, a slop jar next to the bed, a washbowl, a small bar of soap, and a pitcher of water.

"All the comforts of a shanty," Slocum said to himself as he closed the door and lugged his saddlebags over to the bed.

He removed a new bottle of Kentucky bourbon from his saddlebags and placed it atop the bureau next to the pitcher and washbowl.

He sat down and moved the ashtray on his table toward him as he reached in his pocket for a cheroot.

He struck a match, lit the end of the cigar, and waved the match out before dropping it in the simple clay ashtray, which looked as if had been made by a child in kindergarten, what the Mexicans called a *cenicero*. He drew smoke and air through the cheroot and blew the smoke back out the side of his mouth as he looked around the sparse room. There were wooden dowels to hang things on and a couple of Currier & Ives prints that looked as if they had been rained on at some point in their existence.

It was not long before he heard a timid tap on his door.

"It's open," he called out in a loud voice.

The beautiful woman he had seen on the porch opened the door and walked into Slocum's room.

She wore a broad smile on her face.

She was dressed in a tight-fitting dress with a low-cut bodice that revealed her ample bosom. Black net stockings and high-heeled shoes gave a sway to her walk and revealed enough of her legs to catch any man's eye.

"Amy Sullivan," Slocum said. "From Denver."

"John," she cooed. "You remembered me."

She ambled over to the table, and Slocum motioned for her to take a seat in the other chair. He blew the smoke from his cheroot out the side of his mouth again, away from her.

Amy sat down and crossed her legs. Her skirt slipped up to

reveal her garter belt, crimson silk pressing into her soft flesh in a most provocative way.

"Sure, I remember you," Slocum said. "You owned the bar in the Brown Palace Hotel."

Amy laughed.

Her black hair shone even in the lampless drab light of the room. It had a sheen to it that caught light and radiated it every time she moved her head.

"And you owned my favorite bed. I can still hear those old springs sing."

Slocum chuckled at the memory.

"How did you end up in a hellhole like Durango?"

"I go where the money is," she said. "Durango is a boomtown."

"It's where the gold is anyway," he said.

"I've never seen so much gold dust."

"You work at the saloon?" he asked.

"Honey, I run that saloon. Got me a bevy of gals that can shake the gold dust out of a man's pouch faster than you can say 'Jack Robinson.'"

"Greed is such an ugly thing," Slocum said.

"We, the girls, I mean, give fair value for services rendered."

"'To render' meaning to tear apart and rip asunder," he said, a flicker of a smile on his face.

Amy laughed and her laugh was genuine. Her painted lips opened to reveal strong white teeth and the hint of a sensual tongue.

"I can pour you a drink, Amy. Like one?"

She shook her head.

"Pour yourself one if you want."

"Not yet," he said as he drew smoke into his mouth from the cheroot. "I just enjoy gazing at your loveliness."

She patted her hair and smiled.

"Thank you. That reminds me. When we last met in your room at the Brown Palace, we were interrupted. Just as things began to get interesting."

"Oh, yeah, sorry about that."

"A gunman knocked open your door and came in on us. I screamed and fell off the bed. You shot him before he could shoot you."

"I can't forgive him for that."

"I kept the flyer he had in his pocket."

"You did?"

"It offered a reward for your capture and your return to Georgia."

"How much reward?"

"Three hundred dollars."

Slocum laughed.

"It's gone up since then. It's now five hundred dollars."

"Ooooh. You've gotten expensive."

"No, I'm the same price. The reward just went up two hundred greenbacks."

Amy laughed.

"What's your price, John?"

"A kiss," he said.

Amy smiled.

"I can afford that. I don't have to be at work for hours. Maybe we can pick up where we left off. I see that you have a bed."

"And it hasn't been slept in yet. At least by me."

"Or made love in either, I hope," she said.

"It's a virgin bed," Slocum said.

Amy laughed.

"Then it's the only virgin in this room, John."

"I guess it is."

She got up and walked over to the bed. She plopped down on it and bounced up and down. The springs groaned softly.

"Not too noisy either," she said.

"If you say so."

She spread out her arms in a beckoning gesture.

"Maybe it takes two to make it sing," she said.

"You want to hear it sing, Amy?"

She patted the coverlet.

"I'll bet we could make those springs sing a merry tune," she said.

Slocum arose from his chair and walked over to her. He took her hands in his and pulled her off the bed. Then he embraced her in his arms.

They kissed.

The kiss was long and lingering.

He could feel her body ripple under the tight skirt with its slits on both sides. Her kiss was warm and then became wet and hot as they clung to each other.

"Oh, John," she said, breathing heavily, when she broke the kiss, "I want you so much."

"I want you, too," he said hoarsely.

Her hand floated down to his crotch. She squeezed the bulge between his legs. Her touch was gentle as she traced the outlines of his hardening cock balled up in his shorts.

"My," Amy said in a soft voice, "the mister is almost ready. It would not take much to make him stand up."

"No, it wouldn't," Slocum agreed.

She began to unbuckle his gun belt. It dropped to the floor with a thud. Then she attacked his belt buckle, which held up his trousers.

She unbuttoned his pants as the belt sprang free of the buckle. She dipped her hand inside and her fingers roamed his shorts until they touched the flesh of his folded cock.

She pulled it free of his underwear as his pants began to slip from his waist. She squeezed his cock and it unfolded like a switchblade.

Then she dropped to her knees and opened her mouth.

Amy flicked her tongue over the crown of his prick and it hardened even more, the shaft swelling and the veins erupting along its length like blue cords.

She sighed as she took his cock into her mouth. Her tongue flicked and laved the head until it flared with engorged blood. Her head bobbed up and down as she sucked him in and out of her mouth.

Slocum grabbed the back of her head and buried his fingers in her hair. Pleasure shot through him like an electric current as her cheeks became convex and she began to pant as she suckled him to full length.

"You make it hard for a man to resist," he said.

"That's the idea, John."

She fondled his balls and drew on his shaft with a force that made his blood run hot into every capillary.

He squeezed her hair in his hands. Pulled her closer until he was deep in her mouth and touching the back of her throat with the tip of his throbbing cock.

It would not take long, he thought, before he ejaculated and spewed his seed inside her mouth.

But Slocum forced himself to wait.

4

Slocum's trousers slipped down as he thrust into Amy's mouth. She gobbled him ferociously, her head pumping up and down on the full length of his member.

"Do you want it, Amy?" he asked as he felt his seeds boil in his scrotum.

"Uh-huh," she assented and increased her speed.

Slocum gripped her hair and felt the rush of blood through his veins as his passion increased. Her mouth made sucking noises that were louder than the creak of cartwheels, the plop-plop of horses' hooves, and the braying of the mules outside his window.

When he could no longer hold it back, he exploded in Amy's mouth. A surge of pleasure raced through his veins and he closed his eyes. She was ready for it and did not gag when his sperm spewed into her mouth and throat. She gripped his buttocks with both hands and he could feel her fingernails through the cloth of his trousers. She held him inside as he spurted and spurted until he was drained.

The moment of explosion was like a Fourth of July fireworks display in his brain. Colored lights and silver sprays filled the blackness, and every fiber of his body vibrated with pleasure.

She ejected him from her mouth and gasped. She swallowed. She sighed and pulled his trousers down around his ankles before she rose to her feet. She hugged Slocum and whispered into his ear.

"That was wonderful," she said. "You are such a man."

"Best blow job I ever had," he said.

"I loved getting you hard and then sucking you off, John. I'm tingling all over."

He peeled the top of her dress over her shoulders and it slid down. He unfastened her brassiere and her breasts rose and fell with her breathing. He looked at them, admired their symmetry. The nipples stood up and were like tiny faces on the smoothness of her skin.

"I want what we missed out on back in Denver," he said.

"Yes, yes. Can you do it again? So quick?"

"By the time I shuck off my boots and get out of my duds and onto that bed with you, I'll be ready," he said.

"You are an amazing man, John."

"And you are a delight, Amy. Pure pleasure."

He toyed with her nipples. He rubbed a finger over each of them and she squirmed. Her face was flushed and she wiped away the jizm at the corners of her mouth.

They kissed and her dress slid to the floor. She wore red panties with lace trim and he saw the mound of her sex bulge between her legs.

They sat down on the edge of the bed, side by side. He pulled off his boots and took off his pants and undershorts while she removed her shoes and pulled down her stockings. John wrestled his arms from his shirt and tossed it on the floor with his other clothes.

She pulled down her panties and he looked at the dark thatch between her legs. She was beautiful, and when she fell back and dangled her legs in the air, he gazed in amazement at how perfect a body she had, with legs smooth and lean, trim ankles, and painted toenails on her feet as red as cherries.

He rolled onto the bed beside her and ran a hand over her flat tummy. He slid it over the dark wiry hairs of her cunt, and her body seemed to quiver at his touch.

He leaned over and took one of her nipples into his mouth. He rubbed the tip of his tongue over the rough nubbin and Amy squirmed. His left hand probed the portals of her sex. She was wet inside. He touched the tip of her clitoris and she cried out. Her body vibrated as he continued to stroke the little tongue of her pleasure.

"Oh, John, that's so good," she said.

One of her hands reached over and grabbed his shaft.

It was still flaccid, but she kneaded it as if she had a ball of dough in her palm. His cock began to fill with engorged blood as he stroked her clit with his index finger. Soon, his cock began to harden.

Amy cooed with delight.

"Oooh, he's getting ready again," she said. "You are quick, aren't you, John?"

He smiled.

"It's like what the boy rabbit said to the girl rabbit," he said.

"What's that?"

"This won't take long, did it?"

Amy laughed and he rolled over on top of her as he slid his finger from her pussy and released the nipple in his mouth.

She reached down and grabbed his member.

"My, you are ready again, aren't you?" she said.

"Are you?"

"I can take all you've got, John."

He eased down, lowering his hips. She guided his cock through the thicket of her pubic hairs until the crown touched the soft, pliable seam of her cunt. The head slid past her lubricated lips and into the steamy cavern of her pussy. Amy sighed deeply and took her hand away as his cock disappeared into her tunnel.

"Ahhh," she breathed.

Slocum felt his veins throb along the length of his prick as he slid deeper into her.

He slid across the sensitive clitoris and Amy shivered with a rush of pleasurable sensations. When he reached the mouth of her womb, he began to stroke in and out of the moist hot depths and her arms clasped his back. Fingernails dug into his flesh and her legs rose in the air. Back and forth he plunged, with slow even thrusts of his hips and strokes of his cudgel.

"Oh, oh, oh," she whispered and her eyes opened to look up

at his craggy face, his dark wavy hair, the smile of satisfaction curling his lips.

"Sweet," he said.

She bucked beneath him as an orgasm rippled through her pussy and shivered through the muscles of her legs.

"I'm coming," she said.

"You're just flying, Amy. Like a bird."

"Yes, yes. It just keeps on happening."

"Let it happen," he said, and quickened his strokes.

They made love for several more minutes. Amy had to stifle her screams. She thrashed on the bed and dug her fingernails into Slocum's back. He lessened the speed of his strokes and he saw madness flare in her eyes when he went in and out of her with slow even probes. Then, when she relaxed, he screwed her very fast until her body was drenched with sweat and her hair sodden from perspiration.

When it was over, they lay at each other's side, breathing hard. Both of them were oiled with sweat, and the musk of their lovemaking was strong in the room.

"Oh, John, to think that I waited all this time. If I had known, I would have followed you anywhere."

"That would have been a lot of places," he said.

"I wouldn't have cared. You're such a beautiful man in bed. I never had so many climaxes in my life. How do you do it?"

"It's an art," he said. "But it takes two. You're a real woman, Amy. It's your own passion that inspires me."

"That's sweet of you to say that," she said.

"It's the truth. You get what you put into it. And you put in a lot."

She turned over and stroked his damp hair.

"Mmmm," she murmured. "I could want you forever."

"That's a long time, Amy."

"Not long enough for what you give me."

They talked that way for a few more minutes. Then he got up and fished out a cheroot from his shirt pocket, bit off one end, and lit it.

"When I was riding in here this morning," he said, "I saw a man blown out of his mine."

"Oh, no," she exclaimed. "Was he killed?"

"Plumb," he said.

"Do you know who he was? Was it an accident?"

"His name was Wilbur Nichols. And no, it wasn't an accident. It was murder."

"Wilbur, yes. I know him." She paused. "Knew him, I mean. And his brother, Jasper. Nice kid. He'll be lost without Wilbur. Who could have done such a terrible thing?"

"I'd like to find out," Slocum said.

He drew smoke into his mouth and spewed it out in a thin, pale blue stream.

"A woman worked the plunger that blew Nichols to Kingdom Come," he said.

"A woman?"

"Just saw her for a minute. Less than that. She ran off, and then I heard her talking to another woman before they both rode off."

"Did you see the other woman, John?"

He shook his head. "No. They were both in the timber beyond the rimrock by then. I was down on the road. But there were at least two women up there."

"Hmmm."

"Any idea who they might be?" he asked.

"Two women, you say."

"Yes. And one of them is a killer. Maybe they both are."

She thought for a moment. "No one comes to mind right off," she said.

"Any other miners get blown up like that lately?"

She sat up, brushed her hair away from her mouth. She looked down at Slocum and a beam of light shone in her right eye.

"There was an incident a couple of weeks ago. I heard about it at the Mother Lode one night."

"The saloon?"

"Yes. Some men were talking about a friend of theirs, a miner who was accused of raping another man's wife. They didn't mention his name, but I gather these men thought it was a setup, that their friend was the real victim."

"What did they say?"

"I'm trying to think. At first, I thought they were just jawin' like men do when they've had a few swallows of corn whiskey."

"Tell me what you remember," he said.

"They said their friend was lured by some gal up to a cabin or something. Then, when they were both naked as jaybirds, a man busted into the bedroom and threw down on the miner. Accused him of raping the gal. Said she was his wife."

"Then the man who busted in shot the miner?"

"No, not from what they said. They said their friend was pistol-whipped and made to sign some papers."

"What kind of papers?" Slocum asked.

"I don't know. Mining claim, I think."

"And did they say what happened after that?" Slocum asked.

A look came over Amy's face. The blood seemed to drain from her features and turn pasty.

"A few days later, the men came into the Mother Lode again, in a bunch. They looked sad and they didn't raise their voices so I couldn't hear much of what they were saying. But I heard enough to know where they'd been."

"Where was that?"

"To a funeral," she said. "They were just back in from a funeral."

Slocum took the cheroot out of his mouth and his face hardened. A tremor riffled his skin along the jawline.

"What are you thinking, John? I don't know whose funeral it was, or whether it was their friend who died. I wasn't really paying all that much attention. It was a busy night and I had to herd my girls like cattle."

"I'm thinking that their friend fell prey to an old game. The badger game."

"What is that?"

"Gal lures a man to her digs, gets him in the sack, then the husband shows up and demands money. You see it a lot in big cities. The poor souls are usually from out of town and they light a shuck and never press charges."

"How awful," she said.

"Well, it looks like the badger game has come to Durango."

"None of your business, John. Don't get into something you can't handle."

"Somebody has to, Amy. When there's no law, and there is injustice, then someone has to step up and see that justice is done."

"There's not much law in Durango," she said. "But there is a lot of treachery and enough murders to fill up Boot Hill. You should just let matters run their course."

"I saw a man blown to bits this morning," he said. "A man who had every right to live out his days. Someone took that life and I am going to find out who."

"John, it's really none of your business. You don't have a stake in Durango. It's a mining town and people live and die here all the time."

"Amy, I'm a wanted man," he said. "I'm wanted for murder. A carpetbagger judge back in Calhoun County, Georgia, claimed my family's land for himself after the war, and he got it—permanently. I buried him by the springhouse. That's a fact that I can't change right now. But this Nichols man, he deserves better than he got. His soul cries out for justice."

"But it's still not your place to—"

He cut her off.

"Yes, it's my place. I saw it happen. I have to do something for Nichols and maybe a few others who have been swept under the old rug."

She gasped in alarm and hung her head.

Slocum got up and set the cheroot in the ashtray. He began to put his clothes back on while Amy sat there on the bed, her eyes welling up with tears.

"Don't get yourself killed, John. Not now. Not after this. Not after you and me."

Slocum pulled on his boots and thought about the man in the mine, flying through the air, dead as a stone.

And he thought about the women's voices.

If he ever heard them again, he would recognize them.

One way or another, Wilbur Nichols would get the justice he deserved.

Either at the end of a rope, or from the barrel of a gun.

5

Amy dressed quickly. She combed her hair and put on fresh lipstick and a touch of rouge to each cheek.

Slocum watched her dress and felt desire for her all over again.

"Well, I guess this is as good as I'm going to feel all day," she said. She gave Slocum a peck on the cheek. She stood on tiptoes to reach him with her lips.

"There will be other times," he said.

"Promise?"

"I promise," he said. "Before you go, can you give me a starting point?"

"A starting point?"

"A name, or names. Those fellers you overheard in the saloon. I'd like to talk to at least one of them."

"There was only one whose name I knew," she said. "Wally Fowler. He's more of a regular than the others. He's not a miner or prospector. I think he owns a hardware store. Sells mining tools and such."

"Thanks. Know the name of his store?"

"Oh, I think it's Fowler's Tools or something like that."

"Good. That's a start."

"John, I wish you'd stay out of this. I'll just worry about you and get sick."

"I'm not going to stick my neck out. I'm just curious, that's all."

"Ha. You're a town tamer if I ever saw one."

Slocum laughed and kissed her on the lips.

"See you at the saloon later," he said.

"I'll be a nervous wreck until you walk through those batwing doors."

"Don't be. Just take care of your girls."

"I will," she said.

"But don't take the place of any of them."

Amy laughed heartily.

"Never," she said, and then Slocum walked her to the door and opened it.

"Good-bye, John."

"Good-bye, Amy." He locked the door as she walked down the hall. He wanted her again when he saw the bounce of her buttocks.

He found the store owned by Wally Fowler. The sign on the false front proclaimed that it was FOWLER'S MINING EQUIPMENT CO. "Close enough," he said to himself as he walked up to the front door.

Inside, he saw stacks of picks, shovels, adzes, sluice boxes, plowshares, harnesses, boxes of DuPont dynamite, percussion caps, fuses, knives, gold pans, square nails, and assorted pieces of heavy timbers and planking, sacks of concrete, trowels, water jugs, and wooden canteens.

There were two customers in the store and a man arranging items on a shelf behind the counter where sat a bulky mechanical cash register and jars of hard candy. The place smelled of wood and metal and the faint aroma of stale hardtack.

"Help you, mister?" the man behind the counter said as he turned around at Slocum's approach.

"You Wally Fowler?" Slocum said.

"Yep, I'm Mrs. Fowler's boy, Wally. What can I do you for?" Wally grinned at his corruption of the standard customer greeting.

"I wanted to ask you about your friend, I don't know his name, who was caught up in the old badger game."

"What?"

"The man who was surprised with another man's wife or gal friend."

"Oh, that. That's old news. What's your interest?"

"I'm more interested in the gal that got him into that fix and the man who claimed he was being dishonored."

Wally looked askance at Slocum. He was a wiry man, stood about five and a half feet tall in his boots. He wore a faded green shirt and a tattered vest with pencils jutting from one pocket, striped trousers. He had beady eyes and a furrowed forehead that projected over a slightly bulbous nose that was raw around the nostrils from a nasal drip that he wiped every so often with a crumpled handkerchief.

"You ain't the law?"

"No. But I saw a man killed this morning, and I think a gal worked the plunger that dynamited the man from his mine."

"I hadn't heard," Wally said.

"Probably one of your customers," Slocum said. "Wilbur Nichols."

"Wilbur? Hell, I just saw him last night. Had a drink with him."

"Well, you won't drink with him anymore. What I'm trying to find out is who killed him and why, if I can."

"Everybody liked Wilbur."

"Somebody didn't," Slocum said. "That feller who got tangled up with a gal in a badger game. I need to talk to him."

"Why?"

"It was a gal who dynamited Wilbur's mine. Might be a connection there."

"Awww."

"I need his name," Slocum said.

Wally's eyes went wide and rolled in their sockets.

"Man's name is Ed Jenkins. But you can't talk to him."

"Why?" Slocum asked.

"Because Ed's dead. Somebody shot him in the back less'n a month ago."

"Know who killed him?"

"Nope. He was backshot at his mine early one morning."

Slocum thought for a minute.

"He have any kin?"

"Not that I know of."

"So who got his mine, Wally?"

Wally scratched his head.

"Damned if I know. You might check at the assay office down the street. I know Ed filed a claim."

"Any other miners you know who got backshot or dynamited?"

Wally blinked.

"There's always somebody buys the farm up here. It's a rough town. I seen a gunfight in the saloon one night. Two or three men started blasting away with Colts and they carried one of them out, and he was buried next day."

"Miner?"

"Hell, I don't know. Drifter, maybe. Gold brings the bad men to town and they . . . hey, wait a minute. I just thought of something."

"What's that?" Slocum asked.

"A man came to town about four or five months ago. He looked like a gunslinger when we saw him belly up to the bar at the Mother Lode. 'Bout a week later, another'n come in and they acted like they knowed each other. And pretty soon there was a bunch of them. They didn't buy any tools from me. They played cards and kept to theirselves. And one of 'em come in with a pair of pretty gals. I think they was his daughters. But he was one of the bunch all right."

"How many, and do you know the names of any of them?"

"There's a half dozen of 'em. That first 'un what come to town is the leader, I think. They called him Wolf. He's got a face ragged up with scars and wears a red bandanna, sports a pair of Colt pistols on his belt. Wooden grips and they got notches in 'em."

"Just Wolf, huh?"

"Onliest name I heard him called by. They was another'n called Hobart, I think. Hell, I don't remember names when I don't know a feller. But they're a secretive bunch. Stay to themselves and don't buy no drinks for nobody. They go up to the cribs now and then, but never seen them gals since. Both mighty purty, though."

"Do you know the name of the man who brought the gals into town?"

"Clemson, I think. Faron Clemson. He looks meaner'n a bulldog, but don't come out much."

"Thanks, Wally," Slocum said.

"You goin' to remember all them names?"

"Like I grew up with them," Slocum said. He touched a finger to the brim of his hat and walked out of the store.

Wally stared at him for a long time until Roy Cheever, a man who worked in the store, came up to him.

"Who was that, Wally?" the man said.

"I don't know. Forgot to ask him what his handle was."

"He looks like he can take care of hisself," Cheever said.

He was a thin young man with peach fuzz on his cheeks and a hatchet face. He had a tablet in his hand with writing on it.

"I wouldn't tangle with him," Wally said.

"I never saw so much black on a white man," Roy said. "Maybe he's an undertaker."

"No, I think he's probably a gravedigger," Wally said.

"A gravedigger?"

"I mean he puts men in the ground, I think."

"Golly. He don't look like no gunfighter I ever saw. Too polite."

"Don't kid yourself, Roy. That man strikes me as somebody who eats gunfighters for lunch and cleans his teeth with their bones."

Roy's jaw dropped as he watched Slocum vanish from the front window.

He swallowed a gob of saliva and his Adam's apple bobbed under the taut skin of his neck.

6

The sign on the building's front read MINING CLAIMS & ASSAY SERVICES. Underneath was the name ABEL FOGARTY.

The glass door just said OFFICE and underneath it hung a sign that said OPEN.

Slocum walked into a small outer office with a divan, two chairs, a desk, and file cabinets. A slender, attractive woman sat at the desk, her brown hair tied primly back away from a smooth, unlined face. She was poring over printed forms, penning in pertinent data. As he approached her desk, she looked up at him over horn-rimmed glasses. He couldn't tell her age—she could have been twenty-five or thirty-five—but he imagined she'd be even more attractive with her hair down and her glasses off..

"Good morning," she said. She had a pleasant voice. She also had a slender nose and small prim lips that bore little trace of makeup.

"Morning," Slocum said.

"Did you want to see Mr. Fogarty?" she asked. "He's with a client but you're next in line."

"Not if you can help me," Slocum said.

Just then a wooden door with ABEL FOGARTY engraved on it opened, and a small lean man stepped out, followed by an even smaller man with a beer barrel paunch.

"Come back in a week and I'll have that claim ready to file," the second man said.

The first man opened the front door and walked out onto the street.

The second man handed the lady a sheaf of notes written on yellow lined paper.

"Fill out the forms, Clara, and . . ." The man paused as he noticed Slocum. "I'm Abe Fogarty," he said. "Did you want to see me? File a claim? Is Miss Morgan assisting you?"

"I'm just here to inquire about a mining claim," Slocum said. "I don't know if Miss Morgan can help me or if I need to see you, sir."

"Do you wish to file a claim?" Fogarty asked. His pudgy face billowed up over deep-sunk hazel eyes, and his nose was bulbous and sprouted dark hairs out of both nostrils. He wore a gabardine suit that was frayed at the cuffs, and a gold watch chain dangled from a small pocket near the bottom of his faded blue vest.

"Not today," Slocum said. "I'm looking for a claim that might have changed hands recently."

"Oh? Perhaps you'd better come into my office, Mr. . . ."

"Slocum. John Slocum."

"Come this way, Mr. Slocum."

Slocum followed Abel Fogarty into his office.

"Have a seat," Abe said, gesturing toward the center of the room then closing the door.

Slocum sat down in front of a cherry wood desk. The room smelled musty and was surrounded by shelving that contained law books, mining manuals, and large binders with handwritten names on the spines. One wall held a map of Durango and the surrounding lands, while another frame held a map of the entire Colorado territory.

"Mr. Slocum, you're new here, I take it."

"Just rode in this morning."

"And you're not here to prospect or file a claim."

"No."

"That presents a problem."

"Oh?"

Abe swiveled his chair into a half spin as if he had a nervous rear end. It was an annoying habit that irritated Slocum.

"I handle claims, and in the back, I have a man who assays

ore. Our clients demand confidentiality and I honor their wishes."

"I just want to know the name of one man," Slocum said. "I don't want to look at his claim file or know the result of any assay you might have done."

"May I ask who is this man you're interested in?" Abe asked.

"Ed Jenkins," Slocum said without hesitation.

Abe stopped swiveling his chair and stared hard at Slocum.

"Are you talking about the late Edward Jenkins?" Abe asked.

"Yes. He owned a mine or a claim."

"Well, yes, he did. But he died intestate."

"Will you tell me who now owns the Jenkins mine?"

Abe flashed an indulgent smile at Slocum. He made a steeple with both hands and peered over it with that same indulgent smile. He looked like some schoolmaster addressing a child.

"That would be confidential," Fogarty said.

Slocum scooted his chair close to the desk. He leaned over it and lanced Fogarty with green eyes that flashed like gas jets.

"You have a judge here in town, Mr. Fogarty?"

"We do."

"And a sheriff?"

"A constable. What's your point?"

"If you don't give me the name of the present owner of that Jenkins mine, I'll get a search warrant and make a shambles of this office until I find what I'm looking for."

Slocum's jaw was steely as he glared at Fogarty.

"Are you threatening me, Mr. Slocum?" Abe's face flushed and he looked as if he was about to become apoplectic.

"Yes. That's a threat and a promise," Slocum said.

"Well, now, I don't see any harm in divulging the name of the man who's the present owner of that mine. He presented me with transfer papers that were duly signed and witnessed by a notary public."

"That's all I want, Mr. Fogarty, the name of the man who now owns that mine."

"He just transferred the claim last week, in fact," Abe said.

"His name," Slocum said. He leaned tight against the back of his chair.

Fogarty collapsed his steepled hands and got up from his chair. He opened the door and spoke to Miss Morgan.

"Bring me the file I gave you this morning, please."

"Yes, sir, right away," Clara said.

Fogarty returned to his chair behind his desk. He pulled out the center drawer and picked up a slip of paper. He looked it over.

Clara came in with a thin binder and handed it to her boss.

"Is that the one, Mr. Fogarty?" she asked. "It seems in order."

Abe looked at the name on the spine.

"Yes, this is the one. Thank you, Clara."

She left the office without a word.

Fogarty opened the legal binder and looked again at the scrap of paper.

"I've checked the Jenkins signature against the deed transfer," Fogarty said, "and it seems authentic to me. I'm in the process of transferring title to the man he evidently sold his mine to."

"I'm still waiting for the name of the man who now owns the Jenkins mine," Slocum said.

Abe looked down at the folder. "The man's name is Wolfgang Steiner," Abe said.

"Just one man owns the mine now?"

"Yes, that's what I show here. One man. He presented a bill of sale and a document, duly notarized, that Mr. Jenkins signed, transferring ownership to Mr. Steiner."

Abe closed the binder. "Is that all, Mr. Slocum?"

Slocum thought for a moment.

"How many claims does Mr. Steiner own?" he asked.

"Just this one, as far as I know."

"Anyone come in with him when he brought you the papers?" Slocum asked.

Abe swiveled to the left, then to the right, before he answered.

"Just what is your interest in this matter, Mr. Slocum?" he asked.

"Jenkins was murdered. I wonder how many more mines were once owned by murdered men here in Durango."

Abe's face flushed a rosy tint once again.

"I'm afraid I can't help you there, Mr. Slocum. Maybe you'd better talk to Constable Hellinger. He's what passes for a sheriff here in Durango."

"But you know there's something fishy about this deed transfer, don't you, Mr. Fogarty. How much did Steiner pay you to overlook that forged signature?"

"Why, that's an outrageous accusation," Abe sputtered, spitting out a spate of saliva.

"Is it? Your files are confidential. That Jenkins signature could be a forgery. Yet you declared it genuine."

"I examined the signatures. They were exactly alike."

"That's what you say, but Jenkins was murdered and someone else took over his claim. Doesn't that make you suspicious?"

"Why, I—I resent such implications. I want you to leave my office, Mr. Slocum. Now."

Slocum stood up. "I'll go, but I'm going to look into other murders of miners and might just come back with the constable and a search warrant."

"Out!" Fogarty yelled at the top of his lungs.

"I'll be seeing you, Fogarty. Maybe sooner than you think."

Slocum arose from his chair and entered the outer office. He could hear pounding in the room behind Fogarty's office and what sounded like rocks shattering under the blows of a hammer.

Miss Morgan shrank away from him when he appeared in her cubicle. Her face was blanched and her eyes wide.

"Good morning to you, ma'am," Slocum said in a pleasant tone of voice.

Clara's hand went to her throat and she avoided eye contact as he passed close to her desk. He stepped outside and heard Fogarty yelling at Miss Morgan to come into his office.

Something was not right there, Slocum thought. He might have struck a nerve when he accused the man of taking money under the table to overlook a forged signature. Fogarty was a little too secretive to be an honest man.

If there were other murders of miners and titles had changed hands, then Fogarty might be a coconspirator with Wolfgang Steiner and his gang.

Slocum vowed to get to the bottom of the murders and find out just how much Fogarty knew. He wondered now if anyone would take title to Wilbur Nichols's mine.

One thing was certain, he thought as he walked up the street toward the constable's office. If Abel Fogarty was worried, he just might tell Steiner that someone was breathing down their necks.

It would not be difficult to find out.

If Fogarty did warn Steiner, the man would come looking for him.

Such a man might kill to keep a secret.

If so, the wolf could come out of its lair and hunt for him. Such a move would speak volumes about whether or not Fogarty was a criminal.

Slocum had a hunch that Fogarty's hands were as dirty as Steiner's were.

Time would tell.

7

Abner Hellinger stood atop a small stepladder in his office. He held a hammer in one hand and a nail in the other. He held the nail point to the wall and pounded the head into the wood as Slocum opened his office door and walked in. A small bell attached to the door tinkled above his head.

Hellinger turned around and smashed his thumb with the hammerhead.

"Ow!" he yelled, shaking his hand. His face grimaced in pain.

"That will turn black by sundown," Slocum said.

The constable looked around at Slocum.

"What?"

"That thumbnail," Slocum said. "You hit it pretty hard. It'll turn black and might fall off in a week or two."

"Damn hammer," Abner growled. He turned back to the nail and raised the arm that held the hammer. He hit the nail squarely on the head and drove it farther into the wooden wall. He touched the nail.

"Good a damn 'nough," he said, and climbed down from the stepladder.

He set the hammer down on the top step of the ladder and squeezed the hammered thumb in his right fist. He looked up at Slocum. Abner stood a little over five feet in height and wore a badge on his unbuttoned gabardine vest. He adjusted his faded

36

blue suspenders and straightened his thin cotton shirt, which was wrinkled around his waist. His head streamed with strands of black hair over his balding crown. He blinked brown eyes.

"They make 'em tall where you hail from," he said to Slocum.

Slocum did not tell him he was born and raised in Georgia, but he knew that the constable was fishing for that information. He wasn't as dumb as he looked.

"I just got into town this morning. Delivered some horses to Lou Darvin."

"Oh, yes, the freightmaster. Sit down, sit down. Tell me what brings you to my office. Lou short you on the pay for the horses?"

Slocum sat down. So did Abner, in a chair that gave him some height he didn't possess standing up. His desk was strewn with papers. A stack of wanted posters lay on one side and there was a pen lying next to an inkwell. A box two trays high was on the other side of the desk. One tray said IN, and the other one said PENDING.

"No, I got paid what we agreed on," Slocum said.

"Reporting a crime? Somebody rob you?"

"No, not that either."

"Then why would you grace the office of Durango's constable?"

"Those new flyers on your desk?" Slocum asked.

"Matter of fact, I got 'em last week. Haven't had a chance to go through them yet. I get a stack like that about once every month. Useless. A waste of paper. Most wanted men don't come into Durango, which is way off the beaten path. You lookin' for anyone in particular?"

The man was not a dunce, Slocum thought. By any means.

"I wondered if you had a dodger on a man named Wolfgang Steiner," he said.

"Name don't ring no bell."

"Maybe you could look through those latest flyers. He would be recent if he's wanted."

"How recent?"

"Maybe here a month or so. His friends call him Wolf."

"You mean those louts at the saloon," Abner said.

"That's what I heard," Slocum said.

"At the saloon?"

"Nope. Haven't been there yet. I might drop in sometime after sundown."

"What's this man to you? Hey, wait a minute. You're the one who told me about Wilbur Nichols this morning."

Slocum looked at Abner's eyes. They were rheumy and cloudy. The man appeared to be nearly blind.

"Yes."

Abner removed a case from his pocket and opened it. He removed a pair of smoked eyeglasses and put them on.

"Didn't recognize you right off. We drug poor Wilbur's body back to town. He's lyin' on the undertaker's table right now. Pitiful sight."

"He's partly why I'm back here to see you," Slocum said.

"Know the man?"

"No. Never saw him before."

"Oh, yes, you said some gal pushed down the plunger that blew poor old Wilbur clean out of his mine."

"You don't believe me," Slocum said.

"Oh, you probably saw who did it, but more likely it was a young boy, not a woman."

"I know the difference between a boy and a woman, Mr. Hellinger."

"That's Constable Hellinger, Mr. . . ."

"The name's Slocum. John Slocum."

Abner's brows knitted. His eyes blinked behind the smoked eyeglasses. As if he were trying to connect the name to his memory.

"I'll look through this stack of recent wanted flyers and see what we have." Abner picked up the pile of flyers and looked at each one. Slocum saw that he was squinting, even with the eyeglasses. He handed the first sheet to Slocum, and continued this as he went through the pile.

"This one," Slocum said. He held up a flyer and showed it to Hellinger.

"Hmmph," Abner grunted.

Accompanying a drawing of a man's face was a description of him and his crime.

WANTED

FOR ROBBERY & MURDER:

LOBO STEIN: ALIAS LOBO SCHNEIDER

In 1866, the man known as Lobo, along with several cohorts, robbed a stagecoach in Santa Fe, New Mexico. He shot and killed the driver, stole the strongbox containing paper money, coins, and jewelry.

$200 REWARD

Beneath the reward offer were instructions to contact the U.S. Marshals Service in Albuquerque and/or the sheriff in Santa Fe.

"That might be an older drawing," Slocum said. "He probably looks a lot different now."

"Yes. I imagine."

"Have you seen this man?" Slocum asked.

"Not likely. Too many men coming and going here in Durango. Why? Is this someone you know, or used to know?"

"I don't know him, but I think this might be a man who has a gang that preys on miners here in Durango."

"What gives you that idea?" Abner asked.

"The name 'Lobo.' It's the Spanish word for 'wolf.' A man named Wolfgang Steiner took over Ed Jenkins's mine after he was murdered. Filed on his deed and had it transferred to him."

"So what's your point?"

"I think this Steiner is the leader of a gang and might be responsible for the murders of other miners. I have a hunch, a strong hunch, that Jenkins's signature on a Quitclaim Deed might be a forgery."

"That's a serious charge," Abner said.

"Steiner is called Wolf by his cronies. All hard cases. All, perhaps, outlaws. Here in Durango."

"I'm just one man here, Slocum. That would all take a heap of investigating."

"All I need from you is to obtain a search warrant that will allow you and me to ransack Abel Fogarty's files to see how many claims have been transferred from dead men to Wolf and his gang."

"That could take days. Months, maybe."

"There's a time period that would narrow it down. Say claims filed in the last three months or so. Shouldn't be that hard."

Abner stroked his chin with the fingers of his right hand.

"I might be able to get that search warrant, but you'd have to point me in the right direction."

"I have a name or two. I'll get others if I can."

Abner continued looking at the wanted flyers and handing them to Slocum until he had gone through the entire stack.

"That's the lot," Hellinger said. He rubbed his eyes beneath the lenses of his smoked glasses.

"Those help you, Constable?" Slocum asked.

"What?"

"The smoked eyeglasses."

"It's the damned light. From the window yonder. Any light. Hurts like hell."

"But are you nearly blind?"

"Nearsighted. I got some kind of foreign stuff growing over my eyes. Magnifies the light and makes me nearsighted."

"You ought to see an eye doctor," Slocum said.

"Ain't one here in Durango. Nearest one is probably in Denver."

"Your sight is worth a trip up north."

"I reckon. One of these days."

Slocum stood up. "How soon can you get a search warrant from that judge?" he asked as he looked down at Hellinger.

"A day or two, I reckon. Judge Carroway is fond of hunting cougars. Has him a couple of dogs, English pointers, that track 'em. Saw him head out before dawn this morning when I come out of the privy. He lives next to me."

"I'm at the hotel."

"I don't know why in hell you're goin' after lawbreakers in Durango, Slocum, but I guess I ought to be thankful to you for helping out."

"I just don't like to see bad men take the lives of good men. Besides, when I saw Nichols fly out of that mine, it stuck with me. One minute he's digging in his own mine and the next he's deader than a ten-penny nail in an outhouse."

"Must have been a hell of a thing."

"And then there's the mystery, the hidden stuff."

"Mystery?"

"Women can be bitches, and some turn out to be killers. But most of them use poison, and a few of them take up the six-gun. But to dynamite a man takes a cold heart and a heap of nerve."

Hellinger blinked behind his dark glasses.

"Be hell to hang a woman, though."

"Not this one," Slocum said. "She'd make a pretty nice cottonwood flower."

Abner winced at the thought.

"You take care, Slocum. Women have wiles, you know. You can't trust the bad ones."

"No, you can't."

"And stay away from dynamite if you can."

Slocum grunted a good-bye and left the constable's office.

He tried to decide if Constable Hellinger was being funny when he said that last to him. A constable with a sense of humor. Might help. Couldn't hurt.

But there was nothing funny about what he had to do while Hellinger was getting that search warrant.

He would be on his own until then.

Hunting a wolf. A rabid wolf, at that.

8

Faron Clemson sat at the long table with his two daughters, Lacey and Stacey, identical twins in their early twenties.

The room was a converted kitchen and dining room connected to a bunkhouse next door that had been converted into a three-bedroom dwelling. In this room, the stove remained and was still used, along with the dining table and chairs.

The three were eating lunch, consisting of roast beef sandwiches, boiled new potatoes, and cooked turnips.

"You girls did a good job this morning," their father said. "Clean and neat."

"You set up all the wires and dynamite, Daddy," Lacey said. "All I had to do was push down the plunger."

"I was nervous waiting for Lacey with just me and the horses," Stacey said.

"Well, that was a special idea of mine," Clemson said. "I didn't like that guy anyways, and he had his eyes on both of you."

"He gave me the willies," Lacey said.

"Me, too," Stacey said. "But I don't like that kind of thing."

"What kind of thing?" Faron asked.

"Murder," she said.

"Aw, think of your lives ahead, when you're both rich," Faron said.

"That's what you keep promising, Daddy," Lacey said.

"I wonder what Ma thinks about us killing that man," Stacey said.

"Your mother's got ice water in her veins. She don't care one whit. Lord knows, her own hands are plenty dirty."

"You could never tell it by looking at her," Stacey said. "Where is she anyway? I thought she was coming for lunch."

"She'll be here," Faron said.

As if on cue, the door opened and their mother walked in. She looked harried and her gray hair was streaming in all directions.

"You're a mite late, Clara," Faron said. "I'll get you a sandwich."

She sat down in one of the chairs. She and Faron had never married, but she had given birth to the two girls and they had been together for more than twenty years. And they had been on the run for the last ten years.

"I'm too nervous to eat," Clara said. "I'm in a tizzy over what happened at the office this morning."

"Fogarty give you a bad time?" Faron asked.

Her daughters looked at her with questioning eyes.

"No, it was a man who came in snooping around about that deed transfer."

"What man? The law?"

"No, but I think he knows more than he should about Wolf and the rest of the bunch. He asked a lot of questions and forced Abel to produce the transfer papers for the Jenkins mine. He knows the papers are a forgery."

"Who in hell is this jasper?" Faron demanded.

Clara looked at him. Her hands were shaking as they rubbed back and forth on the table.

"Slocum. John Slocum. I don't know why he's asking all these questions. He's not from Durango. He's big and tall and wears all black clothes. He looks mean to me."

"Slocum, eh? Never heard of him. Maybe he's kin to Jenkins."

"No, I don't think so. But he's got something stuck in his craw and I don't think he's going to go away. He could find out about the whole scheme. I think he's going to get a search warrant from the judge and ransack Abel's office."

"He can't prove nothin'," Faron said.

"I just don't know. Abel's sick about it. So am I."

"Well, Wolf's got to know. He's forging papers on that miner we blew up this morning. He won't like it none."

"I'm worried about you girls," Clara said, looking at her daughters. "You might go to prison over this if that Slocum finds out what you did."

"Well, I'm not going to prison," Lacey said. "I'll run first. As far as I can."

"Me, too," Stacey said. "Oooh, I couldn't stand to be locked up in a prison."

"Faron," Clara said, "I think we all ought to leave before this goes any further."

Faron shook his head.

"No need for that. This Slocum feller's just one man. Wolf's got enough guns to get rid of this jasper."

"What if the constable backs up Slocum?" she asked. "And maybe hires on some deputies. Faron, I'm scared. Scared stiff."

"Wolf can take care of Slocum. He don't like folks buttin' into his business."

"Where does it all stop, Faron?" Clara asked. "If Wolf gets rid of Slocum, he might have to kill the constable, too. Then we might get federal marshals in here, and we'll all go either to prison or the gallows."

"Calm down, Clara. We've gotten this far with no trouble from the law. Wolf can get us out of this fix right smart."

"I don't know," she said.

"I think Ma's right, Daddy," Lacey said. "We ought to git while the gittin's good. I never liked the whole idea of Wolf jumping claims."

"And I hate this filthy town," Stacey said. "Wolf's made us into murderers while he sits on his fat ass copying signatures and swilling down whiskey."

"You'd better not say such around Wolf," Faron said. "He's going to make us rich, you'll see."

"Gold won't help us in prison," Lacey said. Stacey pouted and nodded her head.

"Maybe there's a way we can get to Slocum," Faron said.

"How?" Clara asked.

"Set him up like we did with that Jenkins feller," Faron said.

"Oh no," Lacey exclaimed.

"Be easy for a pretty gal like you, Lacey. Or maybe both of you can brace him, then Wolf can bust in and shoot him dead."

Clara frowned.

"That's putting our girls in danger," she said.

"What? For ten minutes of work? If this Slocum is a real man, he won't pass up the chance to bed a couple of good-lookin' gals."

He looked at Clara for support.

She looked at Lacey and Stacey. Tears welled up in her eyes. She wiped them away with dabbing fingers.

"There is a lot of money at stake," she said. "Enough to send our girls to college. That's what I dream of. That's why I go along with your schemes, Faron."

"Then, we'll go to Wolf and tell him how he can get to Slocum. Girls, you'll have to help us out on this."

"Oh, Daddy," Lacey said. "We're not whores."

Faron jerked back as if he had been slapped in the face.

"No, you ain't," he said. "And I ain't askin' you to go the whole way with this Slocum feller. Just get him into bed. Get him drunk if you have to. Then, you both step aside and let Wolf do his work. You can leave before he shoots Slocum so you won't have to see it even."

"I don't like it none," Stacey said.

"Too risky," Lacey said. "We'd have to both play like we was whores."

Faron took a bite out of his sandwich. He chewed it and swallowed before he spoke again.

"No, you just be yourselves," he said to both girls. "You flirt and talk sweet and he'll see that you're not whores, but just two eager girls who want to bed him."

Clara laughed harshly.

"If I were younger . . ." she said.

Faron shot her a scowl.

"Clara, honey, you'd—"

"Don't say it, Faron."

"In your day, you could have any man you wanted."

"This one is quite handsome," she said.

"Oh?" Lacey said, her eyebrows arching like a pair of caterpillars.

"How handsome?" Stacey asked.

"Beautiful handsome," Clara said. "If I was ten years younger, I might—"

"You just shut up, woman," Faron snapped.

He got up from the table and walked to the wall. He took his hat off a peg and slammed it down on his head.

"Where are you going?" Clara asked.

"I got to tell Wolf about this Slocum feller and about how we can get rid of him using the twins."

"You're a cold-blooded bastard, Faron," Clara said. She reached across the table and grabbed a hand from each girl. She squeezed them hard.

"It would only be for a little while," she said. "As a favor to me and your pa."

Faron stalked out of the room.

Clara jumped when the door slammed shut. She released her grip on the girls' hands.

"I'll make it up to you," she said to them. "Buy you some pretties when this is all over."

"Tell us again about how handsome Slocum is, Ma," Lacey said.

"Yes, do tell us, Ma," Stacey said.

Clara smiled at them and patted her hair. She closed her eyes and thought of Slocum and how to put her feelings into words. It would not take much, she thought, for Slocum to stir up the lust in her own heart.

And she wished she were ten years younger.

9

Lou Darvin saw the two men crouching behind a juniper bush behind his building. He held a bucket of feed to take to the horses in the back corral. Jasper Nichols was already out there, working the pump handle up and down to fill the water trough.

Lou felt his heart skip a beat. Something inside his belly froze into a hard cold mass. The two men were looking at Jasper, who did not see them lurking behind the small juniper.

Lou opened his mouth to shout a warning. He took a step toward the back lot, his face ruddy with alarm.

That was as far as he got. His voice never left his throat. Instead, he felt a crushing blow to the top of his head.

His head flopped back and the sky overheard spun in a dizzy whirlpool of blue pinwheels with white clouds caught in the spiral spool.

The pail fell from his hands and struck the ground. Corn and oats splayed from the bucket into the dirt like so much confetti. Then everything went dark as he fell to the ground, knocked out cold.

Grunting, Art Nestor dropped the piece of lead pipe to the ground and walked out into the open. He lifted a hand to signal to the two men in hiding.

Whit Grummon and Bert Loomis both stepped out. They walked with long strides toward Jasper, who could not hear them over the creak and grind of the water pump as he pushed and pulled on the long iron handle.

Slocum entered the large storeroom in time to see Lou crash to the ground and hear the dull clang of the bucket. He saw the man throw down the pipe and raise his hand.

"You there," Slocum called.

Nestor turned and saw the silhouette of a tall man framed in the light from the open door behind him. He wheeled and his hand darted downward for his pistol.

"Back off!" Nestor yelled as his hand pulled his pistol from its holster.

Slocum crouched and his hand was like lightning as it streaked for his .45 Colt. Before Nestor's gun could clear leather, Slocum's pistol was hip-high in his hand and his thumb pressed down on the hammer to cock it.

There was a loud click in the empty storage building and Nestor knew he had a split second to live.

"Damn you," he growled.

Slocum's finger squeezed the trigger and his pistol roared. It spewed smoke and fiery sparks from the muzzle.

Nestor's front sight caught on the lip of his holster.

The lead ball from Slocum's iron slammed into his chest with the force of a sixteen-pound maul. Blood squirted from a split breastbone and drenched Nestor's belly with a crimson stain. He staggered backward. His fingers relaxed and the pistol fell from his hand, tumbling from the lip of his holster.

He hit the ground with a thud, gasping for air from collapsed lungs.

Outside, Whit Grummon and Bert Loomis stopped when they heard the shot from inside the storage building.

Jasper stopped pumping and looked over to see his boss lying on the ground and another man falling backward.

"Get him now," Whit growled at Bert.

Bert drew his pistol and shot Jasper in the back.

Jasper spun around from the force that tore out a chunk of soft flesh from just above his hip.

Whit pulled his own pistol free just as Slocum stepped into view. He saw the tall man in black out of the corner of his eye.

Jasper staggered away from the pump, his hand on his wound, the fingers running red from the gush of blood.

Whit fired at the young man. It was a quick shot and struck Jasper just to the left of his spine. Jasper crumpled and fell to the ground. Pain flooded his senses as his head struck the ground. Dirt and grit lacerated one side of his face.

He groaned in agony.

Whit turned to fire at Slocum, who stepped over Nestor's body and ran toward the two gunmen in a zigzag course.

Whit fired his pistol and he knew his shot would go wild.

The bullet whistled past Slocum's ear and he fired at Whit on the run.

His aim was true. The Colt bucked in his hand, but the barrel held steady when he squeezed the trigger.

Whit doubled over in pain as Slocum's bullet slammed into his abdomen with the force of a pile driver. He grunted and bent over.

Behind him, Loomis stood frozen for a moment. He saw his partner buckle to his knees and his face drained of color. He fired one shot that sizzled over Slocum's head. Then he turned tail and ran down the alley.

Slocum followed him. Loomis turned and took aim, but Slocum was faster, squeezing the trigger of his Colt. His bullet struck Loomis in the left calf.

Adrenaline pumped through Loomis's veins, and he continued to run until he was out of sight. Then the pain caught up with him, and he limped between two buildings and stopped to catch his breath. The pain was intense, but the bullet had gone clean through. He tore a handkerchief in half and stuffed one half in each bullet hole.

Then he tied a bandanna above the wound and limped onto the street, heading for the quarters he shared with Wolf and the other men in his gang.

Slocum reached the dying Whit and looked down on him as a tendril of smoke lazed from the muzzle of his Colt.

"Bastard," Whit spat. His face was contorted in agony and he tried to lift his pistol up to fire at Slocum.

Slocum stepped on Whit's wrist and ground down on it with

his heel. Whit's fingers went limp and the pistol slid from his hand.

"Wolf send you here to do his dirty work?" Slocum said as he gazed down at the stricken man.

"Go to hell," Whit grunted. Blood pumped from a black hole in his abdomen. He grimaced in pain.

"I'll meet you there by and by," Slocum said.

"Who in hell are you?" Whit muttered through his teeth.

"I'm not a boy you can shoot in the back like the coward you are," Slocum said.

"Wolf will tack up your hide on the barn door and set it afire," Whit said.

"He'd better have a big hammer," Slocum said.

"You just goin' to let me die like this?" Whit asked. There was an urgent pleading tone in his voice.

"How do you want to die?" Slocum asked.

"Not slow. Not like this."

"Sometimes a man doesn't have a choice," Slocum said.

He listened to the sound of Jasper's groans a few feet away.

"You gutshot me," Whit said. "No man should have to die like this."

"You're not a man," Slocum said. "More of a snake, likely."

"You rotten sonofabitch," Whit said.

Slocum kicked Whit's pistol away with the toe of his boot. Whit saw it slide through the dirt, out of reach.

"It takes one to know one," Slocum said. He cocked his pistol.

"You goin' to shoot me again?" Whit gasped as a ripple of pain coursed through his body.

"I'm wondering if you're worth another bullet," Slocum said.

"Oh God, the pain," Whit said. His body vibrated with a wave of pain. His abdomen continued to pump blood and his back constricted in the pain from the exit wound.

"Maybe the pain will make you think of that kid you shot in the back," Slocum said. "Why did you do it?"

"I ain't talkin' to you," Whit said.

"No last words?"

"Go straight to hell, mister."

"You give me orders you can't back up," Slocum said.

He didn't know how long the man could live, but his guess was that if he didn't see a surgeon real soon, he would slowly bleed to death and his heart would stop.

He eased the trigger back to half cock and holstered his pistol.

Whit let out a sigh.

Slocum walked over to where Jasper lay. He was writhing in agony.

He knelt down beside the young man.

"Help me," Jasper whispered.

Slocum put a hand on Jasper's shoulder. "Do you know who shot you?" he asked.

"No," Jasper grunted. "N-Never saw him before."

Slocum looked at the two wounds. One was a flesh wound in the young man's side. The other was more serious.

"Get me a doc?" Jasper wheezed.

"Is there one close?" Slocum asked.

"No. Not close. Six, seven blocks, on Arroyo Street."

"I don't think you have that much time, Jasper. I can't stop the bleeding and you've got some damage to your innards."

"I know. I'm real woozy."

Slocum knew, from the pool of blood beneath Jasper, that he had lost a couple of pints. Blood was no longer reaching his brain.

The young man was dying.

"If you know any good prayers, Jasper," Slocum said, "this might be the time to start saying one of them."

"I—I'm dyin', ain't I?"

"You've lost a lot of blood and there's no way to get it back in you."

"I'm dyin', then."

"Yes. I'm sorry, son."

Jasper started to cry. Slocum squeezed his shoulder.

"It's gettin' kind of dark," Jasper said.

"You got any kin in Durango?"

"No. My brother. He was the onliest one."

"Well, maybe you'll see him soon," Slocum said.

He didn't know what else to say. There was no saving the young man. He was pumping out blood in smaller and smaller flows now. His face was blanched almost pure white. His eyes were glazing over, wet with tears.

Jasper tried to turn over to look up at Slocum, but the pain was too great. He slumped even closer to the ground and one of his hands made a fist. A pitiful fist, as if he was trying to hang on a little while longer.

Jasper gasped something, but Slocum could not understand what he was trying to say. The young man closed his eyes and shuddered.

Then he was still.

Slocum leaned down close to Jasper's mouth to listen for signs that he was breathing. Jasper's mouth was closed and so, now, were his eyes. Slocum could feel no pulse when he touched a finger to the big vein in his neck.

Jasper was dead.

Slocum stood up and looked toward the man he had shot.

"Is he dead?" Whit asked.

Slocum did not give him the satisfaction of an answer.

Lou Darvin stirred. He pushed up with both arms and looked over at the dead man nearby.

Slocum heard the sound of a loud grunt and turned to see Lou struggling to get to his feet.

"Mr. Slocum, that you?" Lou called out. He stood up and swayed on his feet. He gingerly rubbed the top of his head and staggered toward Slocum.

"Take it easy," Slocum said.

Whit groaned in pain.

"What the hell happened here?" Lou asked when he saw Jasper lying there and another man lying on his back, bleeding from a hole in his abdomen.

"That man there shot and killed Jasper," Slocum said.

"That's Whit Grummon," Lou said. "We boarded his horse for a few days."

"He's one of Wolf's men," Slocum said.

"Wolf?"

"An outlaw in town."

Lou walked over to Jasper, looked down at him with sad eyes.

"I got jumped," he said. "I wish I could have—"

"Not your fault, Lou," Slocum said. "Jasper never had a chance either. He was backshot."

Lou turned and looked at Whit. Then he strode over to him and glared down at him.

"You're a worthless chunk of shit, Grummon," Lou said.

Slocum walked over to stand beside Lou.

Whit's eyes closed tight in pain. He did not have the strength to reply.

"Let me have your gun, Mr. Slocum. I'll kill this no-good sonofabitch."

"No need, Lou. This sonofabitch is just a sliver and a slice from being cold meat."

Whit's eyes opened.

They were already glazed over and wide with fear. More blood oozed from his wound. Then his eyes closed and he quivered a moment and stopped breathing. His legs shook for a few seconds and then were still.

"He's gone," Slocum said. "There was another man with him. He ran off, but he's toting a lead slug in his leg."

"Somebody's got to pay for what was done to Jasper," Lou said.

"Somebody will," Slocum said.

Lou turned his head and looked into Slocum's green eyes.

"Promise?" he said.

Slocum nodded.

"I promise, Lou."

Then he put an arm around Lou's back and held the swaying man, who seemed about to crumple.

The stench of death was in the air, heavy as a coastal fog.

Slocum knew why they had come after Jasper and killed him.

The young man was the only living heir to his brother's mine.

Now Wolf would have a clear path to ownership of Wilbur's mine. With forged transfer papers, of course.

Slocum vowed that Wolf would never lay claim to that mine or to anything else.

It was just a matter of time.

But he would hunt the man down and call him out.

That, too, was a promise.

10

Wolfgang Steiner listened to Bert Loomis talk about his encounter with a man dressed in black. Bert spoke through clenched teeth while the local doctor, Herman Alcorn, cleaned the wound in his leg.

"The man ain't human," Bert said.

"Hold your leg still," Doc Alcorn said. He held a reeking wad of cotton in one hand, a long slender probe in the other.

"He's human," Wolf said. "And I know who the bastard is, I think."

"Who in hell is he?" Bert asked as he winced in pain.

"According to Abel Fogarty, the man's name is John Slocum. He's been snoopin' around, checking on that claim transfer I filed."

"Never heard of him," Bert said as Doc Alcorn swabbed his wound and poured some yellowish fluid into it.

They were in Wolf's house, a log cabin that had once been the town's first small boardinghouse. Bert lay flat on his back atop a long table in the center of the front room. Tony Hobart sat in a chair by the window nearest the front door. He was on watch, and most of his attention was focused on the front yard and the street outside. The room was Spartan, with no pictures on the walls, a cold fireplace swept clean of ashes, three empty cane chairs, and a sofa where Wolf sat, spinning the cylinder on his converted Remington New Model Army in .44 caliber.

Wolf was hard-muscled and lean, with no fat on his bones. He had a chiseled, square-jawed face, high cheekbones, and a Roman nose. His eyes were wide-set, brown as agates, and seemed to glow with his inner avarice. He was a greedy man and had attained dominance over lesser men because of his willingness to kill anyone who stood in his way. He craved power and money and gathered around him the kind of men who had no conscience and little brain power.

He was already concentrating on how to find this Slocum feller who had killed two of his men and was butting into his business.

The doctor finished cleaning Bert's wound and pushed a salve into both holes in his calf, then wrapped the leg with a soft bandage, tied it tight.

"Stay off that leg for a week or so, Mr. Loomis," Alcorn advised. "If it starts to bleed again, come see me."

"Can you give me something for the pain, Doc?" Loomis asked.

"You shouldn't have more pain than you can bear once the swelling goes down. If your wound doesn't get an infection, you should heal pretty fast. I can give you some pills that will tone down the immediate pain, but take them sparingly."

"It burns like hell, Doc," Bert said.

"That's because I reamed it all out. The pain will go away by tomorrow morning."

"Jesus," Bert said.

The doctor rummaged in his bag and found a small box of aspirin. He poured a dozen pills out and placed them in Bert's hand.

"Take one or two now. Drink lots of water. No whiskey for a week, and stay off that leg."

Alcorn closed his leather bag and walked over to Wolf.

"Two dollars for the visit and the doctoring," Alcorn said.

Wolf dug into his pocket and pulled out a wad of bills. He peeled off two one-dollar bills and handed them to Alcorn.

"Thanks, Mr. Steiner. If he starts to bleed or screams out in pain, you know where to find me."

"Okay, Doc," Wolf said. "I'm betting Bert's not going to need you no more."

"I'll take a look in a few days and change his bandage. See that he stays off his leg as much as possible."

"Will do," Wolf said and holstered his pistol.

Alcorn left and Hobart watched him walk away as he gazed out the window.

"Quack," Wolf said.

"What do you mean?" Bert asked. He turned over on his side to look at Steiner.

"Them sawbones. They're all the same. They act high and mighty, dab on some liniment, and give you some pills that don't do a damned thing."

"You sound like you got some experience with doctors, boss," Bert said.

"I've patched myself up a time or two," Wolf said. "I got no use for a quack sawbones."

"Somebody's coming," Hobart said from his perch by the front window.

"Who is it?" Wolf asked.

"Clemson, I think."

"That peckerhead," Wolf said. "He's got the spine of a jellyfish. I can't stand his constant whining about one thing or another."

"He looks like he's got a weight on his mind," Hobart said.

"Yeah, his hat," Wolf said. "He has the brains of a pissant."

Hobart laughed. Loomis grimaced in pain as he tried to sit up.

"Hobart, help Bert get off that table and into a chair."

Hobart got up and walked to where Loomis was struggling to sit up. He helped him down from the table. Bert leaned on Hobart's shoulder as they walked to a chair. Bert groaned as he sat down. He was out of breath from the effort.

There was a knock on the door.

"Let Clemson in," Wolf said.

Hobart opened the door. Clemson walked in, adjusting his eyes to the dimmer light inside the room.

"What you got on your mind?" Wolf asked.

"That man what's been pokin' around at the claims office, Slocum. I got a way to get to him, Wolf."

"Set down and let's hear it," Wolf said.

"Well, sir, I got my two gals. And they're willin' to put that jasper into, what shall I say, a compromisin' position over at the hotel. Clara's willin' and she'll point him out when he gets back to the hotel."

"Did you know Slocum kilt two of my best men? Put a slug into Bert's leg to boot?"

"Naw, who'd he kill?"

"That's beside the point. Like you said, Slocum's puttin' his nose where it don't belong. So you aim to put your twins up to what? Seducin' that sidewinder?"

"Well, it worked before. My gals are willin' and able."

"Then what? You goin' to shoot Slocum while he's dallyin' with your gals?"

"Well, no. Not me personally. Maybe, when the time's right . . ."

"I don't want to get my hands dirty just yet, Clemson," Wolf said. "There's a man or two I can send over with you."

"That would work," Clemson said. He kept shifting his weight from one foot to another. And his hands trembled slightly as he stood before Steiner.

"When?" Wolf asked.

"Clara wants to do it tonight. When Slocum comes back to the hotel."

"What if he don't?" Wolf said.

"I reckon he has to sleep somewhere. Clara's goin' to find out which room he's in. Then she'll plant my girls in the lobby, all prettied up. Believe me, no man could turn them down."

"You're pretty free with them gals," Wolf said.

"All in your service, Wolf. That's the way we planned it and it's worked so far."

"You got the conscience of a snail," Wolf said. "And the morals of an alley cat."

"Yes, sir. I want to get rich, same as you."

"I'll send Rafe Overton and Jake Snowden with you. But this better work. Slocum's one big pain in my ass."

"Oh, it'll work all right. Just make sure them boys don't shoot my girls."

"Haw," Wolf laughed. "You tell 'em to keep out of the way."

"Oh, I will."

"What are you goin' to do?" Wolf asked.

"I'll keep watch out front of the hotel, and when the gals walk to Slocum's room, I'll send Rafe and Jake after him. After a little wait, of course."

"You go with them, Clemson. Make sure they got the right man. I want Slocum dead as a stone, hear?"

"I hear you, Wolf," Clemson said. "Uh, should I wait around for Jake and Rafe?"

"No, go on over to the hotel. I'll send 'em by after the sun goes down."

"I reckon that's when Slocum will be comin' in," Clemson said. "I don't know where he is right now, but he'll want to clean hisself up some before he hits the saloon after dark."

"You got him figured, have you?" Wolf said.

"No, but Clara has. She knows men like she knows the back of her hand."

"Well, she didn't learn about 'em from you, did she?"

Clemson's face flushed a soft rose and he looked sheepish.

"Clara's had some experiences here and there."

"Yeah, I imagine she has. She's smart, I'll say that for her. Cagey, even."

"Yeah, she is that," Clemson said.

"Well, you better hightail it. Won't be long before that sun drops behind the mountains. You'd better be right about this. I don't want to lose any more men and I don't want Slocum stirrin' up trouble while I'm grabbin' up minin' claims."

Clemson left then, and Wolf snorted as the door closed behind him.

"What do you think, Hobart?" Wolf asked.

"Clemson ain't the brightest spoon in the drawer, but his old lady's smart as a whip."

"I agree. I think Clara just stays with him because she can boss him around. She looks quiet, but that woman's got more balls than a Brahma bull."

"Yeah. She gives me the willies sometimes. She can tame Clemson with just one look. A look like a damned dagger."

"That's why she's at the center of this whole claims thing. Did you know she killed her first husband?"

"No, Wolf, I didn't."

"He cheated on her. She cut him up with a butcher knife."

"How do you know all this?" Hobart asked.

"My older brother, Hans, was married to her."

"Did she get arrested and thrown in the hoosegow?"

Wolf rose from his seat and walked to the window. He looked out at all the buildings across the street, the dark corridors in between.

"No, she didn't," Wolf said as he watched the shadows gather and crawl up the sides of the cabins across the way.

"How so?" Hobart asked.

"She claimed self-defense," Wolf said.

"But . . ."

"It was self-defense. Hans made the mistake of hitting her in the mouth. Puffed up her lips. He hit her again and split her cheek. That's when Clara charged straight at him and buried a knife in his gut, clear to the hilt."

"And you don't hold no grudge against her?"

Wolf laughed.

"Hell no. Hans was a bastard. He was mean and he treated that woman like dirt. Just like he treated our ma. He was no good from the start. I learned a lot from him, but I didn't give a damn that Clara killed him. He deserved it."

"Jesus," Loomis exclaimed across the room.

Wolf turned to him.

"Was that a prayer, Bert, or a curse?" Wolf asked.

Hobart guffawed.

Wolf peered into the dark spaces between each of the buildings across the street. Shadows crawled up the fronts of them and pooled up in between each one like some kind of dark tide.

He had the odd feeling that someone was watching him as he stood in front of the window next to Hobart. But he saw no one. The pane darkened as he watched, and he knew it would not be long until sunset.

"Time to light the lamps," he said to Hobart.

"Want me to stoke 'em up?" Hobart asked.

"No, I'll light 'em. You keep lookin' outside."

There was a strange tone to Wolf's voice as he walked away from the window toward the nearest lamp.

Hobart looked outside. The street was empty.

He thought he saw movement between a log cabin and a clapboard house. Something moved, something darker than the shadows, he thought.

He rubbed his eyes and looked again.

The blob of black was gone.

Spiders crawled all over the nape of his neck.

Had he seen something or someone?

He wasn't sure, and now the sting of a lit match's sulphur crept into his nostrils and he staved off a sneeze.

No need to mention what he hadn't seen to Wolf.

No need at all, because he just didn't know.

11

Slocum made sure that Lou Darvin had regained most of his senses before he headed up the street to follow the blood trail of the man he had winged in the leg.

"Tell the constable I wounded one of the men and I'm going to track him."

"Will do," Lou said. "God, I'm sick about Jasper. Poor kid."

"These killers just didn't happen by here," Slocum said. "Somebody sent them here. I have a good idea who. Now I'm going to prove it."

"How?"

"I have a hunch that the man who got away will run right back to the man who gives the orders."

"Hellinger would like to know who you think is behind this so he can arrest him."

"I think a man named Wolf Steiner sent these backshooters here to kill Jasper."

"Huh? Why? Jasper never hurt nobody."

"Maybe not. But my guess is that he was the only living heir to his brother Wilbur's mine. I think Wolf is just waiting to forge papers to take over Wilbur's mine."

"Good God. This is too much for me to handle."

"Start strapping on a pistol, Lou. With a man like Wolf, nobody's safe in this town." As if to emphasize his advice, Slocum opened the gate on his .45, slid the plunger through the chambers with the fired cartridges. They ejected, one by one, until all three fired chambers were empty. Then he plucked cartridges from his gun belt and inserted them into the empty tubes. He spun the cylinder, pulled the hammer back slightly to half cock, and holstered his pistol.

"Yeah, I might just do that."

Slocum left him and strode to the first spatter of blood glistening the street. That was where he had nicked the fleeing gunman somewhere on his leg.

From there on, there was a clear blood trail up the street.

He noted the boot tracks of his quarry, too, and saw where the man had stopped. Little shards of lint lay on the ground. That told Slocum that the wounded man had ripped up a handkerchief to stop most of the bleeding.

From then on, there was little blood, but the boot tracks were distinct. The man dragged one foot and that left its marks.

He caught up to the man as he went between two buildings and crossed the street.

Slocum saw him limp up to the door of a cabin and pound on it with his fist. A man appeared in the window to see who was knocking. Then the man turned away for a moment. Seconds later, he opened the door.

Once the man was inside, Slocum retreated down the corridor between the buildings, walked to his left, and entered another passageway. He crossed the street, knowing he could not be seen by the man in the window. He hurried between two other cabins and counted two buildings until he arrived at the one the wounded gunman had entered.

He slunk along the side of the cabin toward the front. There were no windows on that portion of the house. He stopped and put his ear to the wall.

He heard talking, but could not make out the words. He moved closer to the front and pressed his ear against the wall near the front window.

Then he could hear every word.

He heard the wounded man speak to another and call him "Wolf."

Wolf called the wounded man "Bert" and "Loomis."

Another man spoke from the middle of the house.

Slocum heard the man called Wolf tell the man to go and fetch the sawbones.

The man he spoke to was named Jimmy John.

Moments later, that man went out through the front door. Slocum listened to his footsteps until they faded from earshot.

Slocum waited, but there was little talk. He heard a table being moved and the stamp of boots by the man at the front window. Then there were groans from someone, probably Loomis, and from the conversation, Slocum knew they had helped him get atop a table.

Some twenty minutes or so later, Slocum heard footsteps scrape on the street. They stopped at the front door.

"Just go inside, Doc. We got a wounded man in there."

"What about you? Aren't you going in?"

"Naw, Wolf wants me to buy him a coupla quarts of whiskey. It looks to be a long night. You go on in, Doc."

Slocum heard a jiggling noise.

"It's locked," the doctor said.

More footsteps as the man with the doctor walked to the window and tapped on it.

"Open up, Hobart. The doc's here."

More footsteps as Hobart went to the door.

"You better go get that whiskey, Jimmy John," Hobart said. "We're dry as camel shit in here."

"I'm a-goin'," Jimmy John said, and Slocum heard his footsteps as he trotted down the street and crossed it.

The doctor went inside.

Slocum listened to the snatches of conversation as the doctor cleaned Loomis's wound, bandaged him up, and then left.

He shrank back against the building, hugged a shadow when he saw a man cross the street at an angle and head for Wolf's cabin.

Later, he heard Wolf call the man "Clemson." He pressed hard against the wall and listened to the entire conversation about the plan to have him seduced by Clemson's two daughters. And he heard the story about Clara and Wolf's brother. Slocum was surprised that the prim and proper "Miss Morgan" had a notorious past.

He had heard enough, so he went back across the street the way he had come and took up his station in the gathering shadows where he could watch the cabin.

The sun was easing down over the high peaks, and soon Slocum was immersed in shadow. He still saw Hobart at the window after Clemson left and then he saw a man come to the window, stand there, and look toward him.

He knew, without ever having seen the man before, that Wolf Steiner was staring straight at him. He could barely make him out, but made note of his features, his clothing, and his build.

Finally, Wolf turned around and disappeared from the window.

When he saw the man who had brought the doctor return with a sack that clanked, Slocum eased back along the shadowed side of the building.

He had seen enough.

He walked back to Main Street and headed toward his hotel.

There were things he knew he had to do before he was approached by the twin girls. It should be an interesting evening, he thought, as he drew a cheroot from his shirt pocket and bit off one end of it.

Somebody, he thought, was going to be mighty surprised.

And it wasn't going to be him.

12

Slocum stopped by a small store that advertised LIQUOR & SUN-DRIES on its front window in blaring red paint. Inside, he bought a quart of Old Mill, a 90-proof Kentucky bourbon. He walked the dark street to the hotel, which was the only building that boasted an outside lamp. Yellow light sprayed from its front windows.

Across the street, under the awning of a darkened theater, The Western Globe, Clara and her daughters huddled in a pool of shadows.

"That's him," Clara whispered to Lacey and Stacey.

"My, he's very tall," Lacey whispered back.

"And very handsome," Stacey tittered *sotto voce*.

They stood in front of a faded poster announcing that Junius Booth was playing the role of Macbeth, a painting of his visage and body dressed in Elizabethan costume.

They watched Slocum slowly stroll into the cone of light from the lamppost in front of the hotel. He paused there for a moment and looked up and down the street. He carried a package under his arm. The cartridges on his belt glistened golden in the spray of yellow light. Bugs and moths flitted around the coal oil lamp and batted their bodies against the gleaming glass.

The women under the shingled overhang stared at the tall man in black, their coats wrapped tightly around them against the chill of evening. The moon had not yet risen and the street was bathed in darkness except for the spot where Slocum stood.

They watched him turn and stride into the hotel.

"This is going to be fun," Lacey said.

"Ummm. I could go for him," Stacey said.

"Hurry, girls. Get across the street and go inside. Smile your prettiest smiles and show him some bare legs."

The girls left their mother and hurried across the street to the hotel as Slocum walked across the lobby to the front desk.

Slocum laid a five-dollar bill on the counter in front of the elderly man who stood there with an expectant look.

"I'm John Slocum. I want another room, but I don't want it on the books. Right next to the one I have. Just one night and you don't give out that room number to anyone who calls. You give out the number of the room I'm now registered in. Just one night. You keep the change."

"Just a moment," the clerk said. He consulted the register and his records. He found the name of John Slocum. "You're in Room 6. I don't have a vacancy next to it, but I do have one directly opposite, across the hall."

"That's fine, Mr. . . ." Slocum said.

"Armand, sir. My name's Jules Armand."

Slocum looked at the man, who appeared to be in his fifties. He was short, thin, with an aquiline nose, and wore a black string tie and a white shirt, striped gabardine trousers.

"From New Orleans?" Slocum asked.

"Yes, sir."

"In the morning, I'll pay for any damages to either room," Slocum said.

"I understand, Mr. Slocum. I'll take you on your word."

Armand handed Slocum the key to Room 7.

"Just remember I'm not in Number 7; say I'm in Number 6."

"That you are, Mr. Slocum. 'Discreet' is my middle name."

"Do you smoke, Jules?"

"I enjoy a cigar now and then."

Slocum fished out a cheroot and handed it to Armand as he slipped the key into his pocket.

"Why, thank you, Mr. Slocum. This was what I smoked down home in New Orleans."

"Enjoy it and think of home, Jules."

Armand smiled. "Indeed I will." Armand looked past Slocum at the front door. He saw two young women enter and loosen their coats. He opened his mouth to say something to them, but Slocum waved a finger in front of his chest to silence the man.

"That's probably the company I'm expecting, Jules."

"They're very young, sir, but also very pretty."

Lacey and Stacey removed their coats and slung them over their arms. They were dressed in ankle-length blue dresses and wore patent leather shoes with straps around their ankles. Lacey wore a pink blouse. Stacey's blouse was mauve. Their rhinestone and turquoise bracelets glittered in the glow of the lamplights.

Slocum walked toward them.

"And twins at that," Jules whispered behind him. *"Sacre bleu."*

"Good evening, ladies," Slocum said.

"Good evening," the girls chorused.

"Are you staying here?" Slocum asked.

"Not yet," Stacey said. She walked up close to Slocum. Her low-cut bodice revealed the rounded contours of her breasts, and her smile was as sweet as a spring sunrise.

Lacey came close on the other side and touched Slocum's arm.

"Will you pet my little pussy?" she whispered, and he gazed down at the mounds of her soft white breasts.

"Does it meow?" he whispered.

Both the girls giggled at his joke.

"It might," Lacey said. "It might bite you, too."

"Follow me," he said. He held out his arms as he held the package in his left hand. The three of them walked out of the lobby and down the hall. Small candles in glass globes lit their way.

Slocum stopped in front of Room 7 and dug the key out of his pocket. He slid it into the slot and turned it. The door unlatched and he pushed it open.

"Oh, it's so dark in here," Stacey said.

"Light us a lamp," Slocum said as he escorted Lacey through

the door behind Stacey, who ventured into the dark room and headed for the nearest lamp on a small table next to the wall.

Slocum and Lacey heard rustling and the sliding cover on a box of matches. Then there was a scratching sound and Stacey held a lit match in her hand. She lifted the chimney and touched the flame to the wick. She slid the chimney back in place and turned the knob that made the wick rise. The lamp grew brighter and light sprayed into the shadows, made them slink away in retreat.

"There, that's better," Stacey said.

"Now, we can get a better look at this gorgeous man. I'm Lacey," she said to Slocum.

"Hello, Lacey."

"And I'm Stacey."

Stacey slunk over to Slocum and batted her eyelashes.

"What do we call you, kind sir?" Lacey asked.

"John," he said. He walked over to the bureau and unwrapped the package. He set out the bottle of bourbon and turned to the twins.

"They gave us three glasses," he said. "You girls like a drink?"

"Sure," Stacey said. "Just a little taste."

"If you're having one, John, I'll drink with you," Lacey said.

The girls threw their coats down on the floor, next to the wall.

Slocum poured bourbon into three glasses.

Stacey approached the bureau and Slocum handed her a glass. She held it to her nose and sniffed.

Then she ran a hand over Slocum's belt buckle, the one that was attached to his gun belt.

"You're a mite overdressed, John," she cooed.

"What did you have in mind, Stacey?"

"I want you to be comfortable. I want to see more of you."

"I want you to pet my pussy," Lacey said. She flashed Slocum an enticing smile.

"Maybe we ought to play strip poker," Slocum said. "If either of you has a deck of cards."

Stacey's hand slid down to Slocum's crotch. She felt the bulge and began to rub her fingers over its contours.

"It looks like you're petting my hound dog," Slocum said to her.

Stacey giggled with delight.

"Ummm. Is he a big dog?" she asked.

"He grows on you," Slocum said. He handed Lacey her glass and sipped from his.

"I'll be he does," Stacey said.

"Maybe we could all sit together on the bed," Lacey said. She sipped her drink and walked over to the bed and sat down on it. She unstrapped her shoes and kicked them off.

"Shall we join Lacey?" Stacey removed her hand and grabbed Slocum's free hand. She led him over to the bed as Lacey began to unbutton her low-cut blouse.

"You girls look pretty young."

"We're old enough," Lacey said. "And we're not virgins, if that's what you mean."

"No, I didn't think you were," he said.

Lacey set her drink down on the nightstand, then took off her blouse. She reached behind her back and began to unsnap her brassiere. She flung it to the floor, and her pert breasts were in full display.

Slocum gawked at them.

"Nice," he said.

"Well, you're still wearing your gun and have your pants on, John. And I still want you to pet my pussy."

"Ever have two girls at once, John?" Stacey asked, setting her drink down next to her sister's.

"I don't kiss and tell," he said.

The twins both laughed as Slocum began to unbuckle his gun belt. He removed it and then buckled it again. He hung it on the bedpost beside one of the pillows.

When he turned around, Stacey removed her shoes and pulled down her skirt. He unbuckled his trouser belt as she slid her panties down her slender legs and let them fall to the floor. He sat down and pulled off his boots, then slid his unbuckled trousers down and kicked them off on the floor.

Lacey finished undressing and lay back on the bed.

Slocum sailed his hat across the room and took off his shirt.

Both girls looked at his male equipment with eyes that grew wider as his cock began to unfurl and extend.

Stacey slid onto the bed, stark naked.

Slocum climbed up and lay between them. He reached over and touched Lacey's dark thatch. Her hips rose to meet his touch, and he slid his index finger into her slit and flicked it up and down.

His shaft hardened and grew longer.

Stacey reached over and clasped his stalk in her hand. She squeezed her fingers together and Slocum's penis grew harder and longer.

"Who's first?" he asked.

There was a sudden silence as the twins looked at each other.

Slocum wondered if they were going to go through with it before there was a loud knock on his door.

He thought that the girls were maybe wondering the same thing.

But there was no knock and he was ready to mount either twin.

13

Stacey leaned over and bent down to gaze at Slocum's manhood. She gripped his stalk gently, her eyes wide with wonder and admiration.

"Can I kiss it, John?" she asked.

"Just don't bite," he said.

Stacey snickered. Lacey squirmed as Slocum fondled one of her breasts. One finger rubbed a nipple and it grew in size.

Stacey took the crown of Slocum's member into her mouth. Her tongue laved the slit and all around the throbbing head of his cock.

Slocum felt the swelling in his shaft as blood engorged it. The veins swelled into blue scrawls all along its length.

"Umm," Stacey moaned as her tongue swabbed over the mushroomed warhead that began to seep precoital fluid. Then she began to suck Slocum's cock, pulling the head into her mouth and sliding her mouth up and down his shaft.

Lacey reached over and pulled Stacey's hair.

"Suck, suck, suck," Lacey said.

Stacey spewed Slocum out of her mouth. Her eyes flashed.

"It tastes good," Stacey said.

"I want you to fuck me, John," Lacey said, pouting.

Slocum patted Stacey on the top of her head.

"Can't do everything at once," he said. "You'll have to take turns." He looked at Lacey.

"I want you inside me, John," she said. "All of it, now that Stacey's slobbered all over it."

"Oh, Lacey, you little bitch," Stacey said. "You always spoil everything."

"I do not."

"Now, now, girls," Slocum said. "Don't fight. Take turns. Lacey, you first. Stacey's already had a small taste."

"That's right," Lacey said. "I'm ready, John. Put that little doggie in my pussy."

Stacey huffed, but she propped herself up on one elbow as Slocum rose above Lacey and lowered his hips to position himself for entry into her pussy.

Lacey reached out and guided him to the mossy portal of her sex. He pushed against her labia and she let go. He slid inside her, slow and easy as Stacey looked on in envy.

"Smooth," Stacey said.

"Shut up, Stacey," Lacey snapped.

Slocum slid up and down her steamy tunnel, and Lacey responded with hip movements of her own. She rose and fell beneath him as his strokes increased in speed. Then she cried out in little gasps of breath as her body quivered beneath him.

"He's giving it to you, Lacey," Stacey said.

"Ummff," Lacey said as she thrust her hips upward, taking Slocum's cock deep within the hot folds of her cunt.

Stacey inserted one of her fingers into her pussy and began to stroke back and forth, stimulating her clitoris with the tip. Her hips began to undulate in time with Slocum's strokes. Her mouth gaped open and her eyes widened as she gazed at Slocum taking her sister on a wild sexual ride.

"Ummm," Stacey intoned.

Lacey gasped with pleasure. Her arms enfolded a large portion of Slocum's back, and she slid her hands to his neck, pulled on it to bring his head down close to her. She kissed him on the lips, and he felt her tongue stab into his mouth and wobble across the tip of his tongue.

Slocum took Lacey up to dizzying heights of pleasure. Her body bucked and rippled with spasms as she climaxed half a dozen times. She cried out each time she reached a climax, much to Stacey's annoyance.

"Enough," Stacey screeched. "Get off her, John. It's my turn."

"Sorry, Lacey," he said. "Your sister is clamoring for attention."

"Oh, oh, oh," Lacey exclaimed. "Go to her, then. I'm floating, John. I'm floating on a cloud."

Slocum withdrew from Lacey and sidled over to Stacey.

Stacey spread her legs and Slocum mounted her. He plunged into her without any need of guidance and Stacey shrieked with delight. He stroked up and down. Her body met his on every rise and fall of his hips. He kissed both breasts, and she clutched at him like a drowning woman.

If anything, Stacey was more eager and more active than Lacey. She thrashed and moaned with each deep penetration, and her fingernails clawed at his back, leaving red streaks that crisscrossed each other like a crude etching.

"Yes, yes, yes," Stacey exclaimed. "Oh, John, it's so good. So very, very good."

Lacey just watched, out of breath and sated. But the excitement of watching Slocum fuck her sister glittered like sparkling diamonds in her eyes.

Stacey climaxed again and again. Each time was more savage than the last, and her legs bobbed up and down like a mad marionette's. She screamed and cooed and clawed like a wildcat. It took all of Slocum's resolve and mental control to keep from spewing his seed into her womb.

She became wetter inside with each climax, and Slocum felt his blood surge into his member, swelling it to enormous proportions. He felt her excitement, and his own pleasure mounted with each stroke, each shattering orgasm that ripped through her loins.

"I'm coming again," Stacey moaned in breathy excitement. "Give it to me, John. Shoot your milk into me. Quick, quick. I want it."

Slocum let himself surrender to Stacey's wild passion.

He sped up his strokes as she clutched him tightly to her breasts. He felt the blood swell in his cock and the jolt of electricity in every fiber of his body. Then he felt that rush of pure pleasure as his seed exploded from his sac and erupted through his penis. He shot into her and Stacey screamed low in her throat as his warm sperm splashed into the deepest recesses of her pussy.

"Oh, yes, yes," she exclaimed.

Slocum floated on a sky filled with brilliant stars and exploding fireworks as he climaxed and spurted his seed into her warm and brothy cavern. He spurted his last, and his diminishing member oozed from her like a dying grub worm.

He lay between the two girls, breathing hard, still enraptured from the dizzying heights of his own orgasm.

Lacey rubbed a hand over his belly.

Stacey entangled her fingers in his long hair.

"That was the best I ever had," Stacey said.

"Don't brag, Stacey," Lacey said.

"I'm full. I feel full. And completed," Stacey said.

"Well, you've used John up, sis," Lacey said.

"Oh, he'll come back, won't you, John?"

He panted his answer.

"In a while maybe."

It was then that he heard footsteps in the hallway. The tromp of boots on thin carpeting.

"Somebody's coming," Lacey whispered and shrank into a mummy of a woman, her hands across her breasts, her legs closed tight together.

Stacey took her fingers from Slocum's hair.

He slid over Lacey and stood up. He reached down and jerked his pistol from its holster.

"What are you going to do, John?" Stacey asked, suddenly afraid.

"Keep quiet," he said. "Both of you."

A thousand thoughts crossed his mind. He tried to count the number of footfalls in order to discern the number of men.

Was it a hotel guest returning to his room or a couple of killers coming to shoot him down?

All he could do now was wait, either for a knock on his door or the sound of a boot kicking it in.

But there was neither.

Instead, Slocum heard the scrape of metal as a key was inserted into his lock.

Slocum cocked his pistol and strode to the dimmest part of the room. He hugged a shadow there, knowing that he still stuck out like a sore thumb.

The lock made a click.

Then he heard and saw the doorknob slowly turn.

A lifetime flitted by in those brief seconds. Both women huddled together on the bed, clasping each other tight, their eyes shadowy and wide with fear.

Then the door slowly opened.

Slocum raised his pistol and sighted down the barrel.

14

Clara shivered in the cold breeze that wafted under the awning. She looked at the glowing windows of the boardinghouse, the saloon, and the hotel, and wished she were inside any of them, where it was warm.

But she had to wait for her husband and whoever else Wolf had chosen to send Slocum to his grave. It seemed hours that she stood there.

And she kept wondering what her daughters were doing up in Slocum's room. Were they just talking and maybe teasing, or were they going to turn into wantons and let the tall man have his way with them?

The thoughts tormented her more than the waiting.

Lately, she had regretted letting Clem—she had always called him that since she'd known him—influence her daughters. She knew that he had not cared for them when they were babies or toddlers. He had never paid much attention to them until they had gotten old enough to work. And that was all he had expected of them. To Clem, they were useful only as laborers, as maids, servants, or of late, enticers of men.

She had been thinking of leaving Clemson, since they were not man and wife, and yet they were bound by something she could not explain. Criminality, perhaps. Some undefinable attraction that had to do with their mutual desire for personal gain, legal or otherwise.

Or maybe Clemson's hold on her had to do with Wolf's brother, Hans, her first and only husband. Clemson had been her salvation after Hans died. He had taken her in when she was ostracized by the whole community. He had shown her some kindness when others had displayed only their cruelty and hatred.

Yet Clem had changed since then, as much as she had. He was no longer the town outcast, the ne'er-do-well who cadged off others. He had become Wolf's brother, in a way, a substitute for Hans.

It was complicated, but she had been trying to unravel all of it ever since they had come to Durango and Clemson had turned her twin daughters into assassins and probably would yet turn them into whores.

Her thoughts were interrupted by the sounds of footsteps coming up the street toward her. She saw three men and recognized one of them as Clemson. Her heart pounded in her chest and pulsed in her temples.

"Pssst," she hissed, "over here."

Clara stepped out of the shadows and waved to the three men. They veered in her direction.

"Clem, over here," she called and waved again.

"I see you, Clara," he said.

The two men followed Clemson to where Clara stood.

"Clara, this here's Rafe Overton and Jake Snowden," Clemson said.

"What you got for us, lady?" Jake asked point-blank.

"He—he's in there," she said, pointing to the hotel. "Slocum, and the girls followed him to his room. Clem, they've been in there for a half hour or so. You're late."

"If he's in there, we ain't late," Rafe said.

"Do what you have to do, but be careful. No telling what my girls are up to with that man."

Jake laughed a harsh and lewd cackle. Rafe snorted.

"Damn you, Clem," she said. "If anything happens to Lacey and Stacey, I'll chop your balls off with a butcher knife."

The two men laughed.

They both were cut from the same bolt of cloth. Jake Snowden was perhaps an inch or two taller than Rafe, but both had beard stubble on their lean, wolfish faces. Both had wide-set pale blue eyes and wore their holsters low and tied tight to their legs with leather thongs. Rafe chewed tobacco and spat a stream of brown liquid that turned amber in the weak light of the hotel lamp. Jake had a burnt-out match in his crooked teeth. They both smelled of whiskey and tobacco smoke.

"Let's go," Rafe said, and spat a wad of tobacco from his mouth.

The three men walked into the hotel lobby and up to the desk.

Jules got up and stood there.

"Good evening, gentlemen," he said politely.

"What room's Slocum in?" demanded Rafe.

"Why he—ah, Mr. Slocum, he's in, let's see, I believe that's . . ." Jules hesitated.

"You better tell us the truth," Jake warned.

Jules looked at the three men and decided his life was more important than keeping his promise to a hotel guest.

"Room 7," he said.

"Give us the key," Rafe demanded.

The elderly man hesitated again. "Uh, I'm not sup-posed to—"

Jake drew his pistol, thrust the barrel close to Jules's face, and cocked it.

"Give me the damned key or I'll splatter your brains all over that back wall," Jake said.

Jules shook with fear. He turned to the wooden plaque on the side wall and removed a key from the spot designated number 7. He handed the key to Rafe, who snatched it from him.

"Just forget you ever saw us," Rafe said.

"You just stay right where you are, pilgrim," Jake said, "and pretend you're deaf, dumb, and blind."

"Yes, sir," Jules said, his face white as a flour sack, fear lighting his eyes with flickers of yellow light from the lamps. As if his fear were painting his eyes.

The three men did not try to soften the sounds of their boot heels on the carpeting as they stalked down the hall with murder in their hearts.

They looked at each numbered door until they reached

Room 7. They halted and each drew his pistol, held their thumbs down on the hammers.

Rafe stepped up to the door and inserted the key. He turned it slowly and heard the lock disengage. He left the key in and twisted the knob.

The door opened and he waited. He turned to look at Jake, who nodded.

Rafe pushed the door open and bent over in a crouch. He thumbed the hammer of his pistol back to full cock and slunk forward into the room, his eyes shifting in their sockets as he gazed right and left.

Behind him came Jake and Clemson. They cocked their pistols.

They all gazed toward the dimly lit bed with its pale coverlet and two naked women drawn up like small statues, their arms crossed over their bare breasts.

One of the women screamed in terror.

15

Slocum heard one of the women scream. The scream was loud and ear-shattering.

He saw the men crouch low and burst into the room.

The scream was cut short when the first man to enter the room fired at the two women on the bed.

Lacey gasped as Rafe's bullet struck her in the chest, just beneath her crossed arms. She fell back onto Stacey, blood bubbling out of her mouth, her eyes wide and glassy with pain.

Slocum fired a split second later. Half of Rafe's face was lit by the spray of yellowish light from the lamp. The bullet ripped into that half of his face and shattered his cheekbone. He grunted and fell to one side as the other half of his head exploded in a shower of blood and shattered bones. He was stone dead by the time he struck the floor.

Behind him, Jake swung his pistol to bear on Slocum, his face spattered with droplets of blood from his partner's fatal wound.

Slocum moved then. He slid along the wall and fired as Jake came out of his crouch and squeezed the trigger.

Jake's shot narrowly missed Slocum, smashing into the wall inches behind Slocum's naked back.

Slocum fired point-blank at Jake. He aimed at his chest and his Colt thundered and belched out flame, sparks, and a deadly lead bullet.

Jake staggered as the ball split his breastbone and tore

through part of his right lung, ripping the sacs to bloody threads. He squeezed the trigger of his pistol as he crumpled onto Faron Clemson's pistol. Jets of blood spurted from the small black hole in his chest, and the fist-sized hole in his back sprayed blood and tissue onto Clemson, who took the brunt of Jake's fall and was pushed backward into the door's frame.

Slocum strode toward Clemson. He cocked his pistol.

Faron stared at Slocum, stunned by his nakedness and the pistol in his hand. He dropped his pistol to the floor and raised both hands in a gesture of surrender.

"D-Don't shoot me, Slocum," Clemson pleaded.

"I ought to blow your damned brains out."

"No, I beg you. I must go to my daughters on the bed. One of them has been shot."

"Who in hell are you?" Slocum asked. He kicked Faron's gun away with his bare foot and held the barrel of his pistol pressed against Clemson's forehead.

"I'm Faron Clemson. I'm their pa. Wolf made me come here."

"Blame somebody else, Clemson. But you knew your daughters were here with me, didn't you?"

"Yes. Ah, it was Clara's idea. Honest."

"You don't know the meaning of honest, you bastard," Slocum said. He wanted to pull the trigger and blow the top of Clemson's head off, but his trigger finger hardened and held still and frozen a hair's breadth from the smooth trigger.

They could both hear Stacey's sobs as she held her dying sister in her arms.

"Let me go to them, please," Faron begged.

"Step toward me," Slocum said.

Clemson took a step over Jake's body, which was still quivering long after he had ceased to breathe.

"Just walk real slow toward the bed," Slocum ordered. When Faron passed him, Slocum rammed the barrel of his pistol into the small of Clemson's back.

"Stacey," Clemson uttered as he reached the edge of the bed. "Is Lacey . . ."

"She's dead, Pa. Lacey's dead." She sobbed and bowed her head.

"Oh no," Clemson cried.

Slocum jabbed the barrel of his pistol hard into Clemson's back.

"You're going to be my messenger, Clemson," Slocum said. He put a hand on the distraught man and spun him around to face him.

"Huh? What?" Faron stammered.

"I'm going to let you live. But only long enough to deliver a message to Wolf. Then if I ever see you again, I'll kill you on sight. Got that?"

"Y-Yes. What—what message?"

"You tell Wolf that I'm coming for him and whichever men he has left. Tell him I'm coming to kill him as soon as I get dressed. Is that clear?"

"Yes, Mr. Slocum. I—I'll tell him. He—he won't like it none."

"How many men does he have left, do you know?"

"Well, there's Hobart and Loomis. Loomis is crippled up where you shot him in the leg."

"Is that all, then? One able-bodied man and the one with the jake leg?"

"Yes."

"And while you're at it, you'd better tell Clara and her boss that they're on my list, too."

"Your list?"

"My list of messes to clean up. You're all crooked as snakes and I've got blood in my eye. Now get the hell out and start delivering those messages while you're still able to draw a breath."

"I'm gone," Clemson said.

"And don't pick up anything on your way out," Slocum called after him as Clemson raced across the room.

When he was gone, Slocum turned to Stacey.

She was bereft with grief. Her eyes were rimmed in red from weeping. She held Lacey in her lap. Lacey was not breathing.

"Stacey," Slocum said, "I'm real sorry."

"Oh you, you are what got my sister killed."

"Blame me all you want, but I didn't shoot her, nor did I want her dead."

"No, but—"

"Just answer one question I have, Stacey, while I get dressed."

"What question?"

"Which one of you pushed the handle of that plunger down at that mine?"

"Who do you think it was?" Stacey said, surprised by his question.

"I think it was Lacey. She was a lot bolder than you. Is that who blasted the dynamite?"

"Oh, what difference does it make now? Yes, Lacey pushed the plunger. I was holding the horses so we could get away afterwards."

"Then there is some sort of justice afoot here, isn't there?"

"You bastard. I hope I never see you again. You killed my sister, sure as if you had pulled the trigger."

Slocum put down his pistol at the end of the bed and began to dress. Stacey glared at him the whole time.

"I'll see that someone comes here and tends to your sister, Stacey," Slocum said as he put on his hat. "You might want to put your clothes back on before the undertaker gets here."

"Go to hell, Slocum," she spat.

Slocum walked to the bureau and picked up the bottle of Old Mill. He walked across the hall and let himself into his room. He locked the door behind him.

He poured himself a drink after he lit one of the lamps.

He waited for the knock that he knew was to come.

He was sorry that Lacey had been killed. He felt sorry for Stacey. But the real culprits were their parents, Clemson and Clara.

And besides those two, there was Wolf and his cronies.

He hoped like hell they would get the message.

If not, he'd have to face them in a death match with high stakes.

Winner take all.

16

Wolf Steiner paced the floor in his dimly lit cabin's front room. Clara sat there on the divan with Abel Fogarty, who was as nervous as a cat in a room full of marbles and rocking chairs. He had his briefcase next to him and a lap full of legal papers that he shuffled through, comparing signatures.

Clara Morgan sat stiff as a board, watching Wolf's angry stride up and down the room. She listened intently to every word, but her mind was back at the hotel. She had deserted her post as soon as Clem and the other two men had entered the lobby.

"Where in hell are those knuckleheads?" Wolf roared. "They've had plenty of time to take care of Slocum."

"I don't know," Clara said.

"Wolf, this signature doesn't quite match Jasper Nichols's. You'll have to do it again or these papers won't go through."

Wolf stopped pacing and wheeled to face Fogarty.

"Damn it. I practiced that signature a dozen times or more."

"Well, it's too far off the mark," Fogarty said.

"Then let Clara do it."

"There's a difference in a woman's signature and a man's," Fogarty said.

Wolf walked over to the two of them. But his eyes were fixed on Abel's like twin jets of burning oil.

"Clara's more of a man than you are, Abel. Let her try it. Nichols's signature is too scrawly for me to imitate."

"That's true," Fogarty said. "It is a difficult signature to imitate."

He turned to Clara.

"Want to try it?" he asked.

Clara snatched one of the documents from Abel's lap and studied the bogus signature. "It's not very flowery, but it does go all over the place. I can try, I guess."

"Do it," Wolf commanded. "Shit."

Clara glared up at him. "Calm down, Wolf, you're going to blow out a blood vessel in your brain."

"Damn those men. Damn Clemson. They should be back by now. I want to know that Slocum's out of the way."

Loomis sat in the chair by the window, where Hobart had been for most of the day. Hobart was back in the kitchen, frying strips of beef in an ocean of melted lard sputtering in a fry pan. He seemed impervious to the squabbles of those in the front room.

"Somebody's comin'," Loomis said. "Just a shadder so far, but he's in one hell of a hurry."

Loomis drew his pistol and held his thumb on the hammer.

"Who in hell is it?" roared Wolf.

"I think it's Clem." He paused for a moment. "Yep, it's Clemson all right."

"Where are the two men I sent with him?" Wolf asked.

"Don't see 'em," Loomis said. "Just Clem, like his pants was on fire."

"Well, let the bastard in," Wolf said.

Loomis limped to the door and lifted the latch. He opened the door as a breathless Clemson jogged up to it.

"Where are the other boys?" Wolf demanded.

He leaned over and gripped both knees with his hands. He panted for breath.

"Dead, Wolf. Slocum shot 'em both," Clemson panted.

"You dumb bastard. Well, get in here and tell me all about it." Wolf glared at Clemson, who staggered over toward the couch. His face was livid, his features drawn.

"Well, spit it out, Clem," Wolf ordered.

"We didn't have no chance, Wolf. Slocum, he was waitin' for us. Buck naked, he was, and he popped off his pistol the minute we come into his room. Rafe, he got off a shot, but he kilt Lacey. Then, Slocum shot him. Jake, he got it, too, and dropped like a stone."

"What about you? How come Slocum didn't shoot you?"

"Hell, he had me cold, Wolf. Stacey was screamin' her head off and Lacey was bleedin' to death. I dropped my gun and put my hands up."

"You lily-livered swine," Wolf growled. "You got the balls of a pissant."

"Shit, he had me cold, I tell you, Wolf."

"So then what?" Wolf asked.

"He gave me a message to give to you, then chased me out of the room."

"What's the message?"

"Slocum said he was comin' after you and he was goin' to kill you."

Wolf snorted.

Fogarty's face blanched as blood fled from his capillaries. He gasped as he choked on sucked-in air.

"He didn't foller you, did he?" Wolf asked. He looked over at Loomis, who had closed the door and was sitting down again. But he wasn't looking out the window. He looked at Wolf and Clemson, wide-eyed as a startled raccoon.

"I reckon not. He was buck naked, I told you. I lit a shuck and didn't look back. But he sure didn't foller me."

Hobart walked into the front room, chewing on the last of his sandwich.

Clara began to sob.

Wolf looked at her with a flash of contempt in his eyes.

"Is—is Lacey dead?" she asked Clemson.

He nodded.

Clara broke down, then buried her face in her hands and wept copious tears. Fogarty patted her on the back with gentleness.

Wolf turned away from Clemson. He shot a look at Hobart, who stood there gape-mouthed, swallowing the last chunk of meat in his mouth.

"What are you goin' to do, boss?" Hobart asked.

"I'm going to kill that bastard. None of you seems able to plug the sonofabitch and put his lamp out."

"How? Where?" Hobart asked.

"Wherever I see him. He comes here, he's a dead man. Right now, I'm thinkin' of goin' to the saloon and havin' a drink. Sooner or later, he'll walk in. You game?"

Hobart nodded. Slowly. Without enthusiasm.

Wolf turned to Fogarty.

"You get them papers signed right, Abel, and put 'em through. Clara, stop your damned cryin' and get to copyin' that signature."

Clara straightened up and wiped the tears from her face with trembling fingers.

"Clem," Wolf said, "you're comin' with us. Where's your gun?"

"It—it's back in that room. Slocum wouldn't let me take it."

"You dumb sonofabitch. Well, I got another in that case yonder. Pick one out that matches your cartridges."

"Do I have to go with you, Wolf?" Clemson asked.

"You damned sure do. If Slocum walks in, you point him out to me."

"Hell, you can't miss him, Wolf," Clemson said. "He's real tall, wears a black hat, black shirt, black trousers, and black boots. He's real noticeable, I swear."

"You're comin', so shut your trap and get yourself a pistol out of that cabinet yonder."

"What about me?" Loomis asked.

"You stay here, just in case, Bert. You see Slocum, you shoot him."

Loomis nodded. He looked sad.

Clara stood up. She looked at Wolf.

"I've seen Slocum," she said. "If I were you, Wolf, I'd saddle up my horse and ride as far away as I could."

"Well, you ain't me, Clara."

"He's already killed off most of your men. What do you want? A big poster with a warning written on it in red blood?"

"I ain't tuckin' tail and runnin' from some no-good drifter with an itchy trigger finger."

"Might be wise to lie low for a while," Fogarty ventured. "I don't feel real safe myself."

Wolf turned to face Abel.

"You run out on me, Fogarty, and I'll track you down myself. Hear?"

Fogarty nodded. "I hear you, Wolf. But I'm not real comfortable with this whole situation."

"Just do your job, Abel. Slocum won't dog us no more once I get him in my sights."

Clemson swallowed hard as he walked to the gun cabinet. He opened the doors and picked out a converted Remington .44 such as he had left in the hotel. He opened the gate and spun the cylinder. It was loaded with six cartridges. He slid the gun into his holster and closed the cabinet doors.

Hobart brushed bread crumbs from his shirt and trousers.

"All right," Wolf said. "Let's hit the saloon. I'm buyin'."

He looked at Hobart and Clemson. Neither were men he would pick to back him up in a gunfight, but he had no choice. Loomis was crippled and these were the only two men who might be able to make sure Slocum went down when the shooting started.

He looked at Clara.

"I'm real sorry about Lacey," he said. "She was a good kid."

"Thank you, Wolf."

"I'm sorry, too, Clara," Clemson said. "I'll make it up to you."

"How?" she asked. "You can't bring her back from the dead, Clem."

Clemson hung his head in shame.

"Let's go," Wolf said and started for the door.

He was building a picture of Slocum in his mind. Tall, dressed in black, and a dead shot. Well, he had come across such men before. They were dangerous, but they didn't have eyes in the backs of their heads. They could be shot in the back as easily as a man could shoot a stray dog.

And he had done both.

17

Less than a half hour after Slocum sat down in Room 6, there was a loud, insistent knock on his door.

A sardonic smile flickered on his lips as he rose to open his door.

"Constable Hellinger," he said as the door widened.

Hellinger's hand was raised to knock again. Beside him stood another man, rotund, with a cherubic face and a rosy-tipped nose, who sported a tin badge on his vest and baggy sharkskin trousers.

Behind them, across the hall, men were removing the bodies. They grumbled and grunted as they laid out canvas stretchers and hefted the bodies onto them.

And Stacey stood beside the constable, tangled auburn hair, lipstick all but worn off, and swollen red-rimmed eyes. Her blouse was askew and her skirt slightly wrinkled. She smiled wanly at Slocum, but he could see that her heart wasn't in it.

Slocum stepped to one side and the trio swept past him. Hellinger was all eyes as he glanced around the room.

"This is my deputy, Elmer Craig," Hellinger said, "and you already know the young lady."

"Have a chair, Constable, Elmer. Stacey, maybe you want to lie down."

"Yes, thank you," she said, a sobbing catch in her voice.

"So far she's cleared you, Slocum. I'm taking her to my office to write out and sign a statement of the events here."

Stacey lay facedown on Slocum's bed, burying her head in the pillow.

"There were three of them. Wolf Steiner's men. I let one go. The father of the two women."

"You know, Slocum, you're filling up the undertaker's shop all by yourself. You're a one-man army."

Slocum shrugged.

Elmer Craig stood by and kept gazing over at the bed, like a watchdog.

"How many more are you going to provide for the funeral parlor?"

"Wolf Steiner is jumping claims all over the place," Slocum said. "He's killed at least two miners that I know of. And he's in cahoots with Abel Fogarty and his secretary, Clara, who's the mother of those twin gals."

"I know, I know. But the law requires proof. And I haven't had the chance to check Fogarty's files to see if he's dirty."

"Oh, he's dirty all right."

"But you ain't the law." Hellinger threw up his hands in exasperation. One of his hands struck the brim of his hat and tilted it off center. He didn't bother to straighten it.

"Justice runs slow sometimes," Slocum said.

"Looks to me like you're takin' some of the law into your own hands."

"Just defending myself."

"Not at Lou Darvin's you weren't," Hellinger snapped.

"One of them cold-cocked Lou and the others shot young Jasper. I call it Citizen Justice. Kind of like a citizen's arrest."

"We got law here," Abner argued. "And I'm it."

"You've got civilization here, Constable. And with civilization, you get both law and lawlessness. When the law's not handy, a man has to become the law."

"That's what you think, Slocum?" Abner was on the border of belligerence.

"That's what I know, Mr. Hellinger. There was no law at Lou's. There was no law across the hall when those men busted in with guns cocked and ready to shoot me."

"That's so, maybe. But Durango's a town, or almost a town, and they hired me to keep the peace and defend its laws."

"If you want to take credit, go ahead," Slocum said. "If you want me to stop defending myself, I won't."

"I don't want you takin' the law into your own hands," Abner said.

"Then you either deputize me, or speed up your investigation of Steiner and Fogarty."

"I got me one deputy, Craig here, and maybe one more I can count on in a pinch, so I go with what I got."

"And you don't need another deputy," Slocum said.

Abner squared his hat and glared at Slocum.

"I don't want a gunslinger wearin' a badge in Durango," he said. "And that's what you are, Slocum, a damned gunslinger, plain as day."

"I'm a horse trader, Constable. But I know right from wrong."

"I ain't goin' to argue with you no more," Abner said. "Next time you're by my office, step in and give me a written account about killin' those men at Lou's and the ones across the hall. Seems to me you knew they were comin' after you, and you just ambushed them before they ambushed you."

Hellinger stood up.

"That the way it looks?" Slocum asked.

"Yep. That's the way it looks at this point. You rented a room across from the one you had and you waited for them men to come after you."

"I knew they were coming for me. I just didn't want a mess in my room."

"Haw," Abner snorted as he got up from his chair. "In the eyes of the law, that's entrapment, Slocum."

"In my eyes, it was a little old ace in the hole, Constable."

"Craig, get the gal. We're goin'," Abner said.

Elmer walked back to the bed and touched Stacey on the shoulder. She turned over.

"Time to go, miss," he said.

Stacey got up and walked with Elmer to where Hellinger stood.

"That little old ace in the hole is goin' to get you killed yet, Slocum. You'll die a cardsharp with a busted flush."

"Good evening, Constable. Mr. Craig." Slocum stood up and then looked at Stacey. "Good luck to you, Stacey," he said. "Again, I'm sorry about Lacey."

"Oh, you . . ." she snarled and turned her back on Slocum.

He closed and locked his door after the three of them had left his room. Across the hall, the last stretcher borne by two men in work clothes left the room with their cargo. One of them carried a sack with pistols that clanked together. They left the door open, and Slocum could see dried blood on the floor.

Slocum waited until there was silence in the hall.

He was in no hurry, but he still wanted to hunt Wolf down and call him out. He knew where he lived now and he went over what he would do in his mind. Wolf would not be easy. But he was running out of guns for protection. No doubt Clemson had given him Slocum's message and he would be ready for whatever came his way.

Well, there was more than one way to skin a cat. Or a snake.

Slocum checked his pistol once again. The cylinder was fully loaded.

He was about to leave when there was another knock on his door. Light taps, such as a woman might make.

His eyebrows arched.

Well, he thought, it was still early. Maybe that was a woman tapping on his door.

He could not imagine who it might be as he walked to the door, unlocked it, and opened it.

There, in the dim light of the hall, stood a woman, all right. But it was the last person he would have expected at that early hour of the evening.

He smiled.

"Come on in," he said.

A thousand thoughts roiled in his mind.

Some of the thoughts were downright lewd.

18

Amy clasped Slocum's shirt when she burst through the door as if she was desperate for him to hold her in his arms.

"John, oh, John, I'm so glad you're still here," she gasped in a breathless rush of words.

"You mean that I'm still alive?"

"Oh, yes, that, too, but I mean here. In your room. Were you going somewhere?"

"I was going to the saloon," he said. He guided her into the room, then closed the door behind her.

"No, you mustn't go there. Not tonight. Not now."

"Sit down, Amy. Try and collect your thoughts."

"I rushed over here from the saloon to warn you," she said as she sat in one of the chairs. She was obviously distraught, Slocum thought, and anxious to warn him of something or somebody.

Amy crossed her legs. She wore a sheath dress with large yellow and green vertical stripes and starbursts of red at the shoulders, a pearl choker, and golden earrings. Her wrists sparkled with silver and turquoise bracelets. Mascara darkened her eyelids and lashes. Her hair was done up in a bun, and a single white gardenia nestled just above her left ear. She looked, Slocum thought, ravishing, with those cobalt blue eyes and cherried lips, dabs of rouge in the hollows of each cheek.

"What's so urgent, Amy, that you had to leave work and run over here?"

"Wolf," she said. "He—he came in a while ago with two other men and looked all around before he sat down."

"That's probably what I'd do," Slocum said.

"One of the men, I know him only as Hobart, went to sit at the bar. He took a seat where he could watch the front door."

"All right. Maybe he wanted his liquor quicker." A smile flickered on Slocum's lips as he sat down in a chair opposite Amy at the table.

"This is not funny," she said, her eyes wide with an admonishing look.

"So then what?"

"Wolf went to a table by the back wall. The other man, Faron Clemson, walked over there with him, but he didn't sit down with Wolf. Instead, he went to a table next to Wolf's, sat down by himself, and faced the front doors. Wolf sat down by himself in a chair that faced the front door."

"Separate tables, eh? Maybe Wolf's expecting more of his men to join him."

"I don't know, but I heard what happened up here and then, a few minutes later, Wolf comes in and he's all eyes, like a tree full of owls. John, I think he's waiting for you to walk in and he, or one of the others, or maybe all three of them, are going to pepper you with hot lead."

"That's the way I might do it, if someone was hunting me and I had men to do some of my dirty work."

"Oh, you," she said. "You're not taking me seriously. All three men ordered beers and none of them had touched their glasses when I snuck out to run over here and warn you."

"Sounds like an ambush to me, Amy."

"So you can't go there, John. Not tonight. They're waiting for you. And they'll kill you."

"I hope you didn't put yourself in danger by coming over here, Amy."

"I snuck out the back door," she said.

"So if I go in the back door with you, where would Wolf be sitting when we enter the saloon?"

"We'd walk through a storeroom, then down a hallway. The

hallway leads into the saloon. Wolf would be sitting at a table to our left. Clemson would be to the left of him at the next table along that wall. The long bar is on our right. At the end of the bar, near the front door, is Hobart, last stool, against the wall. He can see the front door from there and that's about twenty or twenty-five feet."

Slocum pictured the saloon in his mind. Not much different from many he had been in over the years, since leaving Calhoun County in Georgia under a cloud of suspicion and an arrest warrant for murdering a judge. Even though he'd been defending his family farm when he killed the carpetbagger who wanted the land for himself, he couldn't prove it. Yes, this saloon was like places in Dodge, Kansas City, Laramie, Cheyenne. There would be a lot of floor space, in some that served as a dance floor, with tables all around. In others, the space would be filled with card tables where men played faro or poker.

Inside the Mother Lode Saloon, there were three men waiting for him to walk through those batwing doors and into a hailstorm of lead.

Wolf had it all figured out.

Or did he?

In his mind's eye, Slocum made a plan. If he went in the back door, he would not be expected to enter from that direction.

The immediate, and closest, threat would be Wolf at that first table to his left. He might be able to walk right up to him and put a gun to his head. Even if Wolf turned and saw him, Slocum still might have the drop on him.

Hobart would be farthest away, and he would only have Clemson at the table next to Wolf. He might be able to get off a shot if he was fast enough on the draw.

That left Hobart at the end of the long bar. Hobart would have to get up and walk into the open. By that time, Slocum would still have the advantage. Hobart could not shoot through the other patrons at the bar. He would not have a clear shot in any case.

Three men, three bullets.

That was all that it would take, if he was smart enough to outwit three gunmen in the space of a few seconds.

"What are you thinking, John?" Amy asked.

"I'm just going over a game plan in my mind," he said.

"A game plan? This is no game. Those men are there to kill you. All the talk in the saloon is about you and Wolf's men that you killed. This is a small town, and word of those shootings passed from man to man like wildfire."

Slocum's lips curved in a wry smile.

"Well, I know Wolf heard about the last two men of his I shot," he said. "Clemson delivered the message because he was with them, but never got off a shot."

"Clemson was here?" she asked.

"Across the hall. I rented that room because I knew I was being set up."

"With those twin hussies," Amy said in a voice tinged with anger.

"His daughters, I gather."

"That must have been fun for you. The twins, I mean."

Slocum chuckled. "I knew it was a setup, so I rented another room across the hall."

"You're smarter than you look," she said teasingly.

"So are you, Amy."

"Clemson told Wolf you're gunning for him. How does that help you?"

"I wanted Wolf to know that his days are numbered. And I thought my message might bring him out in the open, or drive him out of town."

"Well, you didn't drive him out of town, obviously."

"No. Wolf is probably one of those men who thinks he's invincible. He surrounds himself with backshooters and throat slitters and thinks he's some kind of god."

"I've never seen Wolf come into the saloon by himself."

"Down deep, men like him are cowards," Slocum said. "They're used to running over other people and get a bigger hat size for their swelled heads."

"Still, Wolf's dangerous."

"So is a rattlesnake. That's why you wear boots and step real careful when you're around them."

She reached over and put a hand on Slocum's arm.

"John, why can't you just let all this alone? You don't need to clean up Durango. That's the constable's job."

"One constable. One full-time deputy. Both slower than molasses in January, brainwise and gunwise."

"Still, that's his job. Not yours." She withdrew her hand and sighed as if she knew that her words were falling on deaf ears.

"One of his men shot Lacey. One of the twins. She never had a chance. And he caused the deaths of at least three other men that I know of. If I walk away from this, Wolf will get his way in this town. He'd probably kill the constable and his deputy and have a clear field to rob and kill. Men like him, if they get the advantage, wind up owning the towns they sully. I'd hate like hell to see that."

Amy took on a pensive look.

"So would I," she said.

Slocum squared his hat as if ready to leave.

"What now?" she said.

"I'll escort you back to the Mother Lode. We'll go in the back door and you hide behind the bar so you won't get hurt."

"John, I'm scared," she said.

He stood up. "Don't be. If my plan works, it'll all be over in a minute or two."

"You're that confident."

He took her by the hand and stood her up.

"I am," he said. Then he lowered his head and kissed her on the lips.

She embraced him. The kiss lasted several seconds.

"Umm," she said. "I should keep you here," she breathed.

Slocum smiled. "Let's go," he said, "or I'll forget what you really came for."

She laughed. "You make it all seem so simple," she said.

"Nothing is simple. But you can make things simple if you stick to your guns and walk a straight line."

"I don't even want to think about it," she said.

They walked out of the room and Slocum locked his door behind him. He had thought about taking his belly gun with him, but a six-gun was all he would need. If things worked out, he wouldn't be real close, or use up all six cartridges in his Colt.

They walked to the lobby. It was empty and quiet as a tomb. Jules was not at his desk.

"Follow me," she whispered when they were outside.

They walked past the hotel, then between two buildings to the back alley. In a few minutes they arrived at the back of the saloon.

Suddenly, Amy stopped and grabbed Slocum's arm.

He saw the man as soon as she did.

He stood in the shadows, but he was smoking a cigarette. The tip glowed orange in the dark.

"One of the bartenders?" Slocum whispered to her. They were about thirty yards away and not in the middle of the alley, but closer to the saloon.

"No," she whispered.

"You recognize him? Even in the dark?"

She didn't answer right away. She looked at the man. When he took another puff on his cigarette, part of his lower jaw lit up.

She gripped Slocum's arm.

"I know him," she said. "He's one of Wolf's men. Let's get out of here." There was a tremor in her voice.

Slocum stared at the man. He wore a six-gun. He was definitely on guard.

So Wolf was a careful man. He wasn't leaving anything to chance.

That changed everything. For the moment, at least. His mind raced and he thought about Amy, the danger she was now in.

He pushed her up against the building, then led her to the passageway between the saloon and the building next to it.

"Stay here," he told her in a hushed whisper.

"What are you going to do?"

"I don't know. If I shoot him, Wolf will hear the gunshot and be on the alert."

"He will," she said.

"Who is he? Do you know?"

She nodded.

"His name is Jimmy John. Jimmy John Grimes. And he has a reputation."

"That's good," he said.

She looked up at him, puzzled. She couldn't see his face clearly, but she could see that his mouth was shut tight and he looked determined.

"Why is that good?" she asked.

"A man with a reputation thinks that's a shield that protects him. He thinks that everybody who comes up against him is a coward and will tremble in fear at the very sight of him."

"Most men would," she whispered.

"Not this man," Slocum said. He patted her on the arm. "Stay here," he said. He reached around his side and pulled his knife from its scabbard. Then he stepped carefully and quietly back into the alley.

He hunched low and approached the landing in back of the saloon.

He stalked his prey in deep shadow, silent and invisible.

As silent and as invisible as Death.

19

Jimmy John Grimes puffed on his quirley. He had rolled it moments before and was pretty proud that he had done it in the dark. It was boring out there in the back of the saloon. He would rather have been inside, having a beer or maybe a shot of red-eye.

The smoke stung his eyes and he batted the wisps away.

Slocum stood up a few feet away from the gunman. He held his knife out of sight behind his right leg.

Jimmy John was not looking in his direction.

Slocum took another step until he was within five feet of his quarry.

"Hey, Jimmy John," he said in a voice pitched low and disguised somewhat by his left hand covering his mouth.

"Yo," Jimmy John replied and turned around. "That you, Jake?"

"Yeah," Slocum grunted, and rushed Jimmy John with a single stride straight at him.

"You ain't—" Jimmy John said as he saw the dark figure emerge from the shadows. His cigarette fell from his hand and spewed golden sparks as it touched the boards of the landing.

Slocum brought up the knife. Its blade was just a glimmer in the darkness, but Jimmy John clawed for the pistol hanging from his hip.

Slocum slashed downward, slicing into Jimmy John's wrist. Grimes's hand never reached the butt of his pistol.

He started to yell out in pain, but Slocum smashed him in the mouth with his left fist. Jimmy John staggered backward, off balance.

"Who in hell are you?" Jimmy John muttered.

"Someone you don't want to know," Slocum said and stepped in close as Jimmy John balled his fists. He swung at Slocum.

Slocum threw up his left arm and warded off a roundhouse right. Jimmy John grappled with him, slamming his left fist into Slocum's head just above his ear.

The blow to Slocum's head brought a shower of stars exploding in his brain. Everything went black for a second or two. Jimmy John was stronger than he looked. And a fighter. He felt one of the outlaw's hands groping for his wrist. The hand closed around Slocum's wrist, the one attached to the hand in which he held the knife.

The two men wrestled for possession of Slocum's knife. They rocked back and forth, with neither gaining the advantage. Jimmy John's breath blew hot in Slocum's ear, and Slocum felt the muscular arms of the man as they grappled.

Slocum drove his left fist into Jimmy John's gut. The man had a solar plexus of iron or leather, but it knocked the breath out of Jimmy John and he loosened his hold on Slocum's wrist. Then, Jimmy John chopped Slocum across the bridge of his nose with the edge of his flat hand. Slocum saw stars once again and struggled to keep his knees from buckling under him. He drew his knife backward to deliver a killing stab to Jimmy John's midsection, but the man danced away, out of range. Slocum held the knife steady and circled in a half arc to Jimmy John's left.

Jimmy John doubled up both fists and spread his legs. He half crouched into a fighting stance.

"You got the advantage with that there knife, Slocum," Jimmy John said.

"That's the way I like it," Slocum said. "But I'll give you a choice, Jimmy John."

"A choice?"

"You can walk away, saddle up, and ride out of town right now. No questions asked. Your choice."

"Screw you six ways to breakfast, Slocum. I ain't afeared of you."

Slocum wielded the knife, swish, swish, like a saber in the hand of some ancient warrior.

Jimmy John did not appear to be impressed. He took a step toward Slocum and crouched even lower.

"Your call, Jimmy John. My knife against your fists."

"Grrr," Jimmy John growled and charged straight toward Slocum, flailing first a left, then a right hook aimed at Slocum's head.

Slocum ducked and jumped out of range.

Amy heard the commotion and ventured out from between the two buildings. She looked at the two men and wondered why Slocum was trying to get behind Jimmy John. But Jimmy John was fast on his feet and he turned sharply so that he was still facing Slocum.

She stifled a gasp as Jimmy John drove one of his fists straight at Slocum's face. His left fist.

Slocum swiveled his head sideways to avoid the blow.

That was when Jimmy John's right hand dove toward the butt of his pistol. He grasped the curved wood of his gun grip and began to pull the weapon from its holster.

Slocum knew that if either of them fired a shot, it would bring the saloon patrons out back to see what was going on. And one of them would be Wolf Steiner.

Jimmy John was slightly off balance when his fist missed its target. And his draw was slow. Slocum saw his advantage and swiped at the man's forearm with his knife. The blade cut into Jimmy John's arm. Blood seeped from the gash, and the fingers of his right hand flicked upward so that the grip was no longer fast.

A split second.

Jimmy John grimaced in pain for another second.

"You sonofabitch," he breathed through clenched teeth. He tried to pull his pistol free again.

Slocum leaped a half foot and drove his knife into Jimmy John's left side. The man grunted and twisted away from the blade. Blood gushed through a slit in his side and his breath came hard all of a sudden.

"Bastard," Jimmy John growled.

The pistol was halfway out of his holster when Slocum struck again. This time, he slashed Jimmy John's left arm, high and low. One of the slashes cut through his shirt just below the shoulder, and the other cut the flesh just above the wrist.

Jimmy John backed away. He pulled the pistol free of his holster. He started to raise his arm when Slocum dove into him, butting him in the belly. A rush of air belched from Jimmy John's chest and he staggered a step backward.

But his hand still gripped his pistol and he had his thumb on the hammer to cock it.

That was when Slocum knew he had to finish Jimmy John off before he fired his pistol. He batted at the firearm with his left hand, striking the barrel. The gun swung away from Slocum, and Jimmy John's thumb slipped off the hammer.

Slocum plunged his knife into Jimmy John's chest, just to the right of his ear. The blade sank in deep and Slocum twisted his wrist slightly. The blade widened the hole and ripped out blood vessels and flesh.

"Aw, shit," Jimmy John cried, and his knees began to buckle.

Amy's hand flew to her mouth to stifle a cry. She saw blood spurt from Jimmy John's chest.

Slocum pulled the knife out and rammed it into Jimmy John's belly. He slashed right and left to widen the wound and make hash out of Jimmy John's innards.

Jimmy John dropped to his knees, mortally wounded.

Slocum pulled the knife away and stepped in close.

"Sorry, man," he said. "You made your choice."

Then he slashed Jimmy John's throat in one full sweep of the knife blade. Blood spurted from the wide wound, and Slocum bent his stomach inward to avoid being splattered.

Amy made a sound in her throat and turned her head away at the ghastly sight.

Jimmy John gurgled for a second, fell to his knees, and toppled over onto his face. Blood pooled up where he landed. His legs quivered and kicked spasmodically. He wheezed out a last breath and died in less than a second.

Slocum stepped away and eyed the dead man.

"Wrong choice," he said under his breath.

He stooped over and bent down. He wiped both sides of his knife blade on the back of one of Jimmy John's trouser legs. He stood up and sheathed his blade.

Amy rushed up to him.

"Is he . . ." she breathed.

"He's dead, Amy. Don't look at him."

"I won't," she said.

"Do you feel up to going inside the saloon?" he asked as he held her tight against his body. She was trembling.

She nodded, unable to speak at that moment.

"Gather your wits, then we'll go in."

"I'll be all right," she said. "Just give me a minute."

"Take all the time you want," he said, a tenderness in his voice. He breathed in a large gulp of frigid mountain air. It served to restore his regular breathing and to calm him.

Finally, Amy stood up straight and he released her. She looked up at him.

"I'm ready," she said. "But I'm still scared. And worried. You're walking into a death trap, John."

"We'll see," he said.

"All right."

"You'll go in and look to see if everyone is still sitting in their same places. And if anyone else has come in who works for Wolf. Then I'll watch you, and when you give me a nod, I'll know it's okay to go in. If you shake your head, I'll know someone's out of place, or that I'm more outnumbered than I thought. Got it?"

"Yes. I'll be able to tell right away."

"Then let's go in," he said.

"What about him?" she asked, glancing at Jimmy John's body.

"Either the dogs, the wolves, or the undertaker will be by to take care of Jimmy John," he said.

Amy shuddered at the thought.

They walked through the back door of the saloon, and at the entrance to the saloon itself, Amy left him.

Slocum stood in the dim light of the hallway and watched

her walk over to stand at the lower end of the bar. He saw her look to her left and then down the bar to her right.

He waited to see whether she would nod or shake her head.

He loosened his pistol in its holster and flexed the fingers of both hands.

He knew that Wolf would not be expecting him to enter from that direction. But which man would see him first? Which would be the one who stood up and slapped leather right off?

Whichever one it might be, he was a dead man.

Slocum's jaw hardened as he waited, his gaze fixed on Amy. It seemed an eternity before her head moved.

20

Out of the corner of her eye, Amy Sullivan saw a man enter the saloon, brushing through the batwing doors as if pursued by demons.

She recognized him right away, not only as a patron of the Mother Lode Saloon but as one of Wolf's men, a sycophant who ran errands for him, fawned over him, and kowtowed to Wolf's every whim. He was a scraggly little man who always wore a battered felt hat, grimy duck trousers, and shoddy boots. Now the man held a small wicker basket in his hand. His eyes were wild, his unkempt straw hair streaming from under his hat.

The man was Tom Jessup.

Alarmed, Amy shook her head to warn Slocum off until she could determine what Jessup was doing there with that basket, which she recognized as the kind used by Molly's Café for carryout customers.

Jessup stopped in mid-stride and gazed around the room. Then he headed straight for the table where Wolf sat.

Amy headed that way to overhear what Jessup wanted to say to his boss.

Jessup ran up to the table, his excitement visible. Wolf stared at him with a look of annoyance on his face.

"Boss, boss," Jessup blurted out, "I was totin' this food basket and a pint to Jimmy John out back and he's lyin' dead, his throat cut open and blood ever'where."

"What?" Wolf exclaimed.

"Honest. Jimmy John's plumb dead and he's got cuts all over him. Just lyin' back there in the alley like a gutted shoat."

"Shit," Wolf said. "Sit down and keep your damned voice down."

Amy heard every word. She drifted over to a table where one of her girls sat with three patrons. She smiled wanly at them and patted the girl on the top of her head.

"Are you keeping these gents happy, Maureen?" she asked in a soft tone of voice.

"Yes'm. We was talkin' about gold and minin' and such."

"Well, you fellers enjoy yourselves," she said, and walked over to a spot near the hallway where Slocum was still waiting. Her blue eyes flashed when she saw him.

Slocum held up both hands at his sides as if to ask her what was going on.

"Wait," she whispered.

Slocum heard the word, but also read her lips.

Amy looked over at Wolf and Jessup. They were huddled together, then Wolf stood up and gestured to Clemson, nodded toward the front door.

Clemson stood up.

Wolf walked to the end of the bar and spoke to Hobart, with Clemson right behind him.

Jessup stayed where he was, still gripping the handle of the wicker basket, which rested atop the table.

Wolf, Clemson, and Hobart walked to the batwings and went out into the night. Amy rushed over to where Slocum stood.

"Wolf just left," she said. "And Clemson and Hobart went with him. They're probably going out back to see for themselves what you did to Jimmy John."

"Damn," Slocum said.

"What are you going to do, John?"

"I don't want to face three men in the dark. Let's just see what they do next. I know where Wolf lives. Maybe I can brace him there."

"There's a man still here," she said. "He works for Wolf. Kind of an errand boy. He was to bring a basket of food and liquor to Jimmy John."

"He's still there?"

"Yes, I think he's rattled. He doesn't have much sense anyway."

"Perfect," Slocum said.

He walked into the saloon and looked to his left.

One of Amy's girls was at Jessup's table. He gave her an order for a beer and she walked away, toward the bar.

"That's Wendy," she said. "Tom Jessup just ordered a beer from the bar."

Slocum walked over to the table where Jessup sat. The nervous young man clutched the basket handle as if he was afraid someone would snatch it away from him.

Jessup looked up when Slocum approached. His pale blue eyes were wide and rosy-rimmed from crying, and there were streaks of dried tears on his face.

"Jessup," Slocum said.

"Yeah, that's me. Tom Jessup."

Slocum sat down and looked into the little thin man's eyes.

"Do you know who I am?" Slocum asked.

Jessup shook his head. But his hands began to tremble and his eyes darted in their sockets like wayward marbles.

"I'm John Slocum. And I'm the man who put Jimmy John's lamp out a while ago."

"Jesus," Jessup blurted out.

"Is that a prayer or a curse word?" Slocum asked.

"I—I know who you are now, Slocum. I seen what you done and I told Wolf."

"You work for him." It was not a question.

"Yes, I'm beholden to Wolf. He's my boss."

"I'm not going to hurt you, Tom, so just relax."

"I—I can't. My nerves is janglin' like a bunch of windmills in a big old blow."

Amy went to the bar, where she spoke to Wendy.

"Don't take that beer over to Tom Jessup," she said. "He won't be here long."

The barkeep set an empty beer glass down.

"What? Oh, I get it," Wendy said. "Joe, hold the beer," she said.

"I already have," Joe said.

Amy smiled and stepped a few feet away to look at Slocum and Jessup at the table. Jessup's face was all bone from lack of blood. Whatever Slocum was saying to him, she thought, it was scaring Jessup half to death.

"I mean you no harm," Slocum said. "But I want you to deliver a message to your boss, to Wolf. Can you do that for me? His life and yours depend on you giving him my message."

Jessup nodded until Slocum thought he might dislocate his head from his neck.

"Wh-What message?"

"I want you to tell Wolf that if he doesn't ride out of town tonight, with all his men, he'll never see sunrise."

"I can't tell him no such thing," Jessup said. "You don't know Wolf. He don't scare and he might beat me to a pulp."

"If you don't deliver that message, Tom, you won't see tomorrow's sun come up either. You'll be lyin' on the street like your friend Jimmy John. I mean it."

"Golly, mister, you're askin' a whole hell of a lot."

"You want to help your boss, don't you?"

"I reckon. But that's a mighty dangerous message."

"Just tell him it's from me, John Slocum. He won't hurt you."

"I reckon I can do that. I don't want to die. Not like Jimmy John."

"I'll be watching you, Tom. Every step of the way. I know where Wolf lives and I'll come in there and kill him and everyone else if he doesn't saddle up tonight and light a shuck out of Durango."

"Jesus," Jessup said again. He let loose of the basket handle and wiped sweaty palms on his trousers.

Slocum stood up.

"Now, get to it, Tom. I'll be right behind you. But you won't see me. Just think of Jimmy John back there in the alley with his throat cut and stinking to high heaven in his own blood."

"Christ," Jessup said and stood up.

He edged away from the table. He left the basket where it sat and ran toward the door. Then he scampered through it, his shirttails flying.

Amy walked over to Slocum.

"What did you tell him?" she asked.

"I told him to warn Wolf to get out of town or I'd kill him and all his men, including Jessup."

"My God. Wolf won't back down. John, he'll come after you and kill you. Shoot you in the back."

"If he comes after me, that's fine, Amy. My bet is that he will lay low for a time, then try for me."

"You think he'll just ride out of town?"

"Oh, he won't go far. And I'll be right on his tail."

"If he goes into the timber, that's thousands of acres. He can hide and pick you off from most anywhere."

"I've hunted all kinds of game, including wolves and mountain lions, Amy."

"They didn't have guns."

"No, but they didn't have horses either. And horses are a sight easier to track."

"I'll worry about you," she said as Slocum started to leave.

"Tell the constable I said howdy if he comes in," he said.

Slocum walked to the batwing doors and out into the chill night air.

He would give Jessup time to walk the few blocks to Wolf's house, then he'd take up a position where he could see what Wolf's next move was. He had ignored Slocum's previous message.

Maybe this one would have the desired effect.

Or maybe the sight of Jimmy John lying dead in back of the saloon would finally get through to him.

Blood, he reasoned, spoke louder than words.

21

Wolf struck a match as he bent over the body of Jimmy John.

"That murderin' bastard," he gruffed. "Look at what he did to Jimmy John. Probably snuck up on him in the dark and slit his throat, the sonofabitch."

"There's scuff marks all around, boss," Hobart said.

Clemson gagged at the ugly sight of Jimmy John's slashed throat and the copious amount of blood pooled up under his head.

Wolf's match went out and he struck another. He went over the landing and saw that Hobart was right. The dirt was roiled and there were partial boot marks. He traced the marks away from the landing. He struck more matches and began to piece together what had happened to Jimmy John.

"A woman brought Slocum here," he said. "He did sneak up on Jimmy John from twixt them buildings. They likely tussled some before Slocum did his dirty work with his knife."

"Jimmy John would have put up a hell of a fight, all right," Hobart said.

Clemson stepped away from his vomit and wiped his mouth. His stomach was still queasy and he stank of stale beer.

"Yeah," Wolf said as his last match went out. "He put up a hell of a fight, but his knife is still on his belt."

"So is his gun. Still in his holster. He fought the bastard bare-handed."

Hobart knelt down and unbuckled Jimmy John's gun belt with the knife and pistol holster attached.

"Jimmy John was a damned good man," Wolf said, a bitter tone to his voice.

"The best," Hobart said.

"Well, we know who did it," Clemson said in a scratchy voice. He could not look at the dead man, but just stood there, pulling in gulps of air. He could taste the sour beer still.

"Slocum, no doubt," Wolf said. "Question is, who was the woman who led him here? One of the saloon girls, maybe."

"Maybe," Hobart said. He buckled the gun belt and slung it onto his left shoulder.

Wolf thought back to the time when the three of them had entered the saloon. In his mind, he recounted each move that he and the other men had made.

Hobart had walked to the end of the bar and stationed himself there as his first lookout. He and Faron had walked to the tables at the wall and each taken separate ones. He remembered ordering from Wendy and she had taken Clemson's order as well. Maureen was somewhere in the middle of the room, bowing and curtseying as she greeted regular patrons. The bar was lined with several men who were jabbering to each other and to Joe, the barkeep.

Amy Sullivan had nodded to him, but had not stopped by his table. She'd stood near the bar, looking over the house.

When he had looked again, he didn't see her. She was gone. He assumed she had gone to the ladies' room to use the chamber pot and dab powder on her nose.

She had been gone a long time.

When he saw her again, she stood near the bar as before, but seemed more alert.

Then Tom had come in and he had lost track of Miss Amy Sullivan. He had paid her no attention, but something in the back of his mind told him that she had disappeared again. She was a striking figure, with her beauty and that dress in the colors of the Mexican flag.

"Do you think Clara might have told Slocum about Jimmy John being out back?" Hobart asked. "She was the only other one who knew."

Wolf growled in his throat.

"No, it wasn't Clara. I think I know who told Slocum. Let's get to the house. I have to, by God, think all this through."

"If not Clara, then who, Wolf?" Hobart asked as the three of them left the landing and walked up the alley toward Wolf's cabin.

"I'll keep that to myself for now. But it was damned sure a woman. You can't trust any of them."

Just then, a block away from the saloon, they saw a man run out from between two buildings and dash up the alley.

Wolf knew who it was. He called out.

"Tom," he yelled, "where you goin' in such a hurry?"

The man stopped and peered at them through the darkness of the unlit alley.

"Wolf, that you?" Tom called out.

"Yeah."

"I was just goin' to see you. I saw him, Wolf. I damned sure saw him."

Jessup ran toward them on awkward, seemingly disjointed legs.

Wolf held out both arms to stop him in case he tried to run over them.

"Whoa, Tom, whoa up there," Wolf said. "Who did you see?"

"That man. Slocum. He come into the saloon."

"Don't jabber, Tom. Take it easy and tell me what you saw."

"He come up to me at the table. Big man. Tall, all dressed in black."

"So?" Wolf kept walking. He dragged Tom along with him.

"He give me a message, boss. I told him I didn't want no message, but he said if I didn't give it you, he'd kill me."

"What's the message?" Wolf stopped in his tracks. The others stopped, too.

"He said he's a-comin' after you. But he says for you to haul ass out of town and he won't bother you none."

"Another threat, eh?"

"Uh-huh," Tom said.

Wolf started walking again, pushing Tom ahead of him.

"That all, Tom?"

"He said you got to go real quick."

Tom looked over his shoulder as if to see if anyone was following them.

"He was real mean and real sure about it," Tom said.

"All right. Calm down, Tom. I'll take care of it."

"Boss, you gotta hurry and get out of town. He's a-comin', I tell you."

Hobart choked off a laugh. Clemson gagged on some leftover vomit in his throat. He bent over and choked it up, spat on the ground.

"What do you think I ought to do, Hobart?" Wolf asked, holding on to Jessup was like handling a boneless marionette. Tom wriggled and danced a jig as they walked along.

"We ought to bushwhack the sonofabitch. Teach him what's for."

"Faron, you got any ideas?"

They crossed over to the next street. Light glimmered on the window of Wolf's cabin. They could all see the silhouette of a man at the window, Loomis.

"Might be best to light a shuck and lay low for a few days," Faron said. "Maybe Slocum will just go back where he come from."

"Yeah, that's not a bad idea. Slocum don't live here. He's just a drifter. But he's stickin' in my craw and murderin' everybody I know."

"You mean you'd turn tail and run, Wolf?" Hobart said.

"For a while, maybe. Give me time to think."

"What if he follows us?"

"We could bushwhack him like you said. Plenty of hiding places up on the mountain."

"That's true," Hobart said.

They reached the house. Loomis pressed his face against the window. Wolf waved to him and Loomis sat back down.

"Tom," Wolf said. "You delivered the message. Now git and find yourself a hidey-hole until all this boils over. Likely Slocum won't come after you. I mean, he let you go, didn't he?"

"Yeah, he did. I'm goin', boss. I hope I never see that man again."

Wolf laughed and watched Tom run off toward the stables on his skinny legs. He didn't expect to see Tom anytime soon.

Loomis opened the door.

"Howdy, boss," he said, seemingly with great relief.

Wolf and the others swept by him.

"Anybody been by?" Wolf asked.

"Nope. It's dead quiet around here."

"Good."

"What're you goin' to do, Wolf?" Hobart asked.

"First, I'm going to pour myself a drink of whiskey, then I'm goin' to reconnoiter," Wolf said.

"What's that 'reconnoiter'?" Hobart asked.

"Take a look at the situation and decide what to do next," Wolf said as he walked to the kitchen, where he kept his liquor in a cabinet.

"Boss," Faron called out, "I'm goin' home. Lessen you need me."

"Naw, go on, Faron," Wolf said as he opened a cabinet with a squeaky door. There was the sound of clinking bottles as he reached for one of them.

Hobart walked to the kitchen.

"I'd like a taste myself, Wolf," he said.

Wolf took two glasses from the cupboard and set them on the sideboard. He filled the glasses almost full.

"There you go," he said as he handed one glass to Hobart.

"You trust Clemson, Wolf?"

"About as far as I can throw this cabin," Wolf said. "Why?"

"I think Faron's goin' to light a shuck. The man's about to pee his britches right now. Every time Slocum's name is mentioned, he jumps half a foot inside his skin."

"I know. He's always been that way. A born coward if there ever was one. He's got a spine made of raspberry jelly."

"Why keep him around, then?"

"I've got reasons."

"Mind sharin' 'em?" Hobart asked. The two walked into the front room.

"He's my stand-in with Clara," Wolf said.

"Huh?"

"He keeps watch over her for me. He and Clara ain't hooked up. Never were."

"I thought . . ."

"That's what I want everybody to think. Clara's always been my woman, but I never wanted anybody to know about her and me. We go back a long ways, her and I."

"I never would have guessed," Hobart said.

"That's the way I wanted it. Clara's useful, but I don't trust her much. You know, women are devious sluts at heart. Treacherous. They're like elephants, too."

"Like elephants?"

"They never forget nothing. They carry a grudge long after it's wore out."

"I never saw . . . I mean, you and her never, you know, acted like you were real close."

"You mean you never saw us hug or kiss or see me take her to my bed."

"Well, yeah. None of that."

Wolf sat in his easy chair. Hobart took a place on the divan.

"Whatever I once had for that woman is long gone," Wolf said. "But Clemson keeps an eye on her for me. You know the old sayin', 'Keep your friends real close and your enemies even closer.'"

"Yeah, well, is she your friend or your enemy?"

Wolf smiled. "Let's just say that Clara and I share a secret, and as long as she's alive, that secret's safe. She does what I say and I keep my distance."

"Do you hate her, then?" Hobart asked.

Wolf looked up at the beamed ceiling.

"No, I don't hate her. I just know what she is and what she suffers in her mind. She's got a companion she can talk to, Clemson, but she don't tell him what's really on her mind. He plays his part, and she plays hers."

"I don't understand none of it," Hobart said and swallowed some whiskey from his glass.

"It's beyond anyone's understanding, my boy." Wolf drank. "Except mine," he said.

He was already thinking about something else and the conversation died out like a wind that rises and falls into stillness.

He was thinking about Slocum.

Maybe, he thought, he should lie low for a while. Take to

the timber and let Slocum fret and then leave town and go about his business.

The more he thought about batching it up in the mountains, the more he liked the idea.

And tonight would be an ideal time to leave town and find a place to hide until Slocum coughed up whatever was in his craw.

22

Stacey was still sobbing when her mother came into their cabin. She sat up on the couch and looked at her mother.

"Did you . . ." Stacey started to say.

"I saw her, Stacey. Mr. Monsanto brought in his cosmetologist, Peggy Mendoza. She's very good and is making Lacey look as pretty as possible."

Clara laid her purse on the table in the dining room. There was a grim, haggard cast to her face. Her eyes were rosy from crying, and there were small tracks of tears still on her face.

She sat down and put her arm around her daughter. She gave her a loving squeeze.

"Thanks, Ma. I feel so terrible about what happened to Lacey. I wish I had been the one who got shot."

"There, now, Stacey. You can't change what happened. It was Fate. Or maybe it was God's will. You're alive and you must go on. No matter what happens to us in life, we must go on. You and I will keep Lacey in our memories and someday we'll all see each other again."

"You mean after we're dead," Stacey said.

"Yes, but I believe some part of us lives on. Maybe in Heaven, maybe in some far-off paradise where God makes everything right."

"I wish I could believe that."

"Well, it helps if you believe in something, my daughter. If

I didn't think I'd never see Lacey again, I would just give up.
But I won't give up. And that's what has kept me strong all
these years, ever since you were born. I think we have to have
something beyond ourselves, beyond the miseries of life, so
that we can help and teach others. I want you to believe that
you and Lacey will be together again and that you will always
be happy. Life is so hard, there has to be something better."

"I never thought of it that way, Ma."

"I've made terrible mistakes and I have to think that someday I will be able to look back and know how I could have
changed things in my life. Especially the bad things."

"Oh, Ma, I love you so much. You've been so kind and loving to me and Lacey. I just wish she was still here."

Clara took her arm from around Stacey's back and stood
up. She walked to her bedroom. Stacey followed her. Clara
went to the wardrobe and began removing clothing from the
pegs, her trousers, a heavy chambray shirt, a sheepskin-lined
leather coat, boots, and a gun belt with a small .38-caliber
Smith & Wesson revolver in a holster.

"Ma, what are you doing? Where are you going?"

"Lacey was the last straw. I'm going to do something I
should have done a long time ago."

"What?"

"Kill Wolf Steiner. Or help Slocum kill him."

"You can't be serious, Ma."

"Oh, I'm serious all right. I never told you the whole story
or even most of it, but I've lived with it all these years." She
paused and looked at Stacey as she began to unbutton her
blouse. "Honey, go make us some coffee, will you. Then I want
to tell you the whole story, one I've kept from you since you
were old enough to understand."

Stacey looked puzzled.

"I'm almost afraid to hear what you are going to say, Ma."

"It will clear up a lot of doubts you may have had all these
years and know why I made you and Lacey do such horrible
things."

"Well, sure. I've had a lot of doubts and a lot of questions.
But I never questioned you, Ma. I knew you were . . . well, that
you were just trying to help us all out in life."

"Make that coffee, darlin'. I won't be long."

"Ma, you're scarin' me now, with that gun and all."

Clara smiled wanly.

"I'm a good shot. But I've never killed anyone before."

"But Wolf? He's a dangerous man. A killer. And he's mean."

Clara waved a hand at her daughter.

"Shoo," she said. "I'm in a hurry, but there are things you have to know before I go."

"All right, Ma, but I don't like it none."

Stacey left the room.

The door was still open, so Clara could hear her daughter walk down the hall to the kitchen. Could hear her banging the coffeepot and the stove lid, opening the firebox, and putting kindling in it.

She stripped off her skirt and shoes, her stockings. She dressed in gray riding pants and the chambray shirt, put on heavy woolen stockings, and slipped into her riding boots. Her trail togs, she called them. She left the jacket on the bed and walked back into the living room.

A few minutes later, Stacey came into the room. "Fire's going and the coffeepot's on the stove. It'll be boiling pretty soon." She gave her mother a measuring look.

"That's what you wore when we rode here to Durango. Where's your pistol?"

"I'll strap on my gun belt just before I leave."

"Where are you going?"

"I'm going to try and find Mr. Slocum. But first, I'm going to pay Abel Fogarty a visit and tell him I've quit my job with him."

"Wolf made you go to work for him anyway, Ma."

"I know. Wolf wanted me there. Part of his damned scheme."

"But you did it."

"Stacey, we'll talk over coffee. I'm nervous as hell and I need something to calm my nerves. And I need these few minutes to collect my thoughts."

"Sure, Ma. I'll see if the water's boiling yet."

Stacey left the room and Clara could hear her in the kitchen. She heard the cupboard door open and the rattle of cups and saucers.

Her mind was a tangled briar patch of thoughts. There were so many things on her mind at that moment that she had difficulty sorting them out. There was Abel Fogarty, of course, and Slocum. She hoped she could find him. If not, she'd have to go to Wolf's cabin by herself and speak her mind before she shot him dead. She wondered if she had the courage to do such a thing. Lord knows, she had thought of it often enough. But Wolf was a dangerous man and he had dangerous men around him. Still she forced herself to put down her fears and would die, if need be, to rid the world of the monster who had ruined her life.

Stacey entered the room with a small wooden tray and two cups and saucers, a small coffeepot that was spewing steam from its spout. There was also a bowl of sugar and two spoons. She set the tray down on the small table in front of the couch and sat beside her mother.

"Do you want to pour, Ma, or should I?" Stacey asked.

"I'll pour. You just sit back and listen to what I have to tell you."

Clara poured brewed coffee into the cups.

"Sugar?" she asked.

Stacey shook her head.

Clara spooned sugar into her coffee and stirred it. Then she sniffed the hot liquid, and blew on it before she drank. She leaned back as she swallowed her coffee.

"What did you want to tell me, Ma?"

"I guess I should just start at the beginning, or maybe at present and then go back to the beginning."

"You sound so mysterious, Ma."

Clara laughed. It was a nervous laugh. And she had to quell the shaking that was starting with her fingers.

"First of all, Stacey, Faron Clemson isn't your father. Did you ever wonder?"

"I wondered why you and him didn't act like man and wife. He didn't act much like a father either. Lacey and I talked about it some. We just thought that was the way it was for people who've been married a long time. But we knew you weren't married to him. You just tried to act like you were married sometimes."

"Faron was just as much a prisoner as I was. Maybe not walled in, or shackled, but prisoners nevertheless."

"How so?" Stacey asked.

"Now to the beginning, Stacey," Clara said.

Stacey sipped her coffee and waited for whatever was to come from her mother.

"When I was young, I was attracted to a boy. Hans Steiner. He had a twin brother, Wolf. They were identical twins, but I could tell the difference. Hans was a gentler soul, and he had a sense of humor. He made me laugh. And he was very tender. We planned to get married as soon as we were out of school. But Wolf was attracted to me, too. And he was very jealous of Hans. In fact, he tried to break us up and he fought with Hans more than once."

Clara took another swallow of her coffee. Stacey scooted to the edge of her seat.

"Wolf asked me to marry him," Clara continued. "I refused. He told me I'd be sorry. He said he was more of a man than his brother would ever be."

"That's terrible," Stacey said.

"It gets worse. Hans and I were both seventeen years old. We got married in secret, but Wolf found out about it. My parents had given us a little cottage on their property and that's where we went after the preacher joined us in matrimony."

"But I guess Wolf found out where you were living," Stacey said. "Did he, Ma?"

"He found out. Hans carried me over the threshold, and that night, when we were getting ready to consummate our marriage, Wolf came into our cottage."

"Oh no," Stacey exclaimed.

"He had murder in his eye, and he cursed Hans and then killed him. He raped me on what was to be my marriage bed. He raped me all night while Hans was lying dead in the front room."

"How horrible," Stacey said. She looked stunned. And she was.

"He did it to me over and over. I was in shock. I couldn't believe all that was happening to me. I thought I had to be dreaming a bad dream."

"But you weren't, were you?"

"No, it was all too real."

"Then what happened, Ma? Didn't Wolf want to marry you?"

Clara took a deep breath. She set her cup back down in its saucer and sighed.

"No, Wolf did not want to marry me. He hated me for picking Hans to be my husband instead of him. He said he'd never marry me and that I would never marry another man as long as he lived. He made me go with him, and he left town and began his outlaw life. I had to tag along, and he had his way with me whenever he pleased, but there was no man to satisfy my longing to be loved and cared for. When you girls were born, he made Faron act as father to you, but told him if he ever so much as touched me, he'd kill him."

"So we grew up thinking that Faron was our father," Stacey said, "when Wolf was our real father."

"That's the way Wolf wanted it. I felt sorry for Faron, but he's a spineless weakling. I kept hoping someone would come along and save me from my fate. I wanted a champion to take up my cause and wipe out all the ugliness and torment in my life."

"But nobody ever came," Stacey said in a dull tone of voice. She sat there in shock, buried under the weight of this new knowledge.

"No one, until I saw John Slocum," Clara said.

"Slocum is your champion?"

"He might be. The minute I saw him, I knew he was the one I had been waiting for."

"Yet you gave him to me and Lacey."

"My gift to both of you. I know I'm not young and pretty anymore, and I just wanted to live a dream through you and your sister."

"My God, Ma, I can't believe you. You're still young and pretty. I think Mr. Slocum would want you."

"Hmm," Clara said, "I wonder. I could be pretty again if I wanted to. But I think most of my life has passed by. I just want to believe that there is a good man around and Slocum is my idea of that good man."

"But he's a gunfighter, Ma. Just like Wolf and his henchmen."

"But for good, Stacey, for good. Not evil, like Wolf. Wolf made me do things, not only to myself, but to you and Lacey."

"I know," Stacey said. She looked and felt sad.

"He said he'd have me arrested for the murder of his brother if I didn't do *everything* he asked. He'd tell the sheriff he actually saw me kill Hans." Clara sighed and got up from the couch. "I'll be right back," she said.

Stacey sat there and waited.

When Clara returned, she had her gun belt around her waist and her jacket under her arm.

"I'm going, Stacey. I hope I get back in one piece, but if I don't, I want you to know I love you very much."

"Don't say that, Ma. You'll be back."

"I hope so. But if I'm not, make a good life for yourself, my sweet daughter."

Clara embraced Stacey when she stood up. She kissed her on the cheek and patted her on the head.

"Good-bye, Ma," Stacey said as her mother put on her coat and walked out the door.

"Good-bye, Stacey."

Clara sighed with relief as she walked toward Abel Fogarty's home the next street over from hers.

Then she would go to the saloon, and if Slocum wasn't there, she'd try to see him at the hotel. And if she did not, she would go to Wolf's and play out the rest of her hand. But it wasn't a game, she knew. It was life or death. She was glad that she had told Stacey the whole story, had finally gotten to tell someone the truth of what had happened to her twenty years ago.

This, she told herself, was something she should have done a long time ago, long before they had all come to Durango.

Her daughters had been caught up in her life of crime, and one of them was dead. Now all she had was courage and determination.

The past was past. There was nothing she could do to change all that had happened. But if her hunch was right, there would be a future. She hoped and prayed that her hunch was right.

And as if Fate had answered her prayers, she saw someone emerge from Fogarty's cabin. Someone she had not expected to see.

For coming out of the house, dressed all in black, was the man she had picked to be her champion.

"Good evening, John Slocum," she said in an artificially merry voice.

"Is that you, Miss Morgan?" he asked as she drew near.

"Call me Clara, please," she said.

"Clara, then. I just told your boss that his days were numbered, and if he was smart, he'd hightail it out of Durango before something bad happened to him."

"He's not my boss. I was coming here to tell him I had quit and that I would testify against him in a court of law when he was arrested."

"Well, well, well," Slocum said. "A woman after my own heart. And I see you're dressed to ride out yourself."

"I want to ride with you, Mr. Slocum." She opened her coat so that he could see her cartridge belt and her pistol.

"My, my, will wonders never cease," he said. "Will you take my arm? I think we have a lot to talk about before the night is over."

"Yes, I think we do," she said.

"My hotel?"

"Perfect," she said as she slipped her arm inside his.

They walked, arm in arm, to the hotel like a couple off to do some spooning in the moonlight.

They both wore smiles on their lips.

23

Slocum picked up his room key from Jules, who was still rattled over the deadly disturbance in the hotel.

"There won't be any more trouble here, will there?"

"I don't expect any," Slocum said. He ushered Clara down the hall to his room, number 6, and opened the door to let her in. He locked it after he had entered.

"Have a seat, Clara," he said. "Make yourself comfortable. Drink?"

He walked to a lamp on the table, struck a match, lifted the chimney, and touched the lighted match to the wick. The room took on a soft peach glow that reached to their table.

"No thanks, John," she said. "I need my wits about me."

"Seems to me you're never without them. How's Stacey?"

"I told her the whole story about her and Lacey's birth and who her father really is. I don't think it has all sunk in yet. But she's all right. Or seems to be."

"Who is her father? Not Clemson?"

"No, not Faron. I might as well tell you the whole story, too, and tell where I've been all these years and where I am now."

"I'm all ears," he said. He took off his black hat, set it on the third chair.

Clara told him all about Wolf and his twin brother, Hans, what happened on her wedding night and the brutal hold Wolf had on her that had lasted for twenty years. She told her story in a rush and then sighed with relief that she had gotten it all out.

"But" she said, "I'm interested in what you told Abel Fogarty."

"I told him that he had a short time to live if he stayed in town and filed forged documents on any mines where the owners were murdered by Wolf and his gang of cutthroats."

"Good," she said. "What did he say?"

"He turned as pale as a bowl of hominy grits and said he'd light out in the morning and close his office."

"Do you think he will?" she asked.

"One of his balls is the size of a pea, and the other is a real itty-bitty one," Slocum said with a curve of a smile on his lips.

Clara laughed.

"You're all right, John Slocum. Do you know that?"

"Nope. I don't judge myself much. I leave that to other people."

She reached across the table with both hands. Slocum took them in his.

"You're packing iron," he said. "Were you going after Wolf by yourself?"

"If I couldn't find you, I was," she admitted. "I've been his prisoner all these years, and after Lacey died, I just knew I had to get away from him."

"You were going to kill him?"

"Yes, unless I found you."

"You wanted to find me?"

"Yes, I knew you were not afraid of a mean bastard like Wolf and I was going to side with you."

Slocum chuckled. "Still, you're pretty brave. What if you hadn't run into me?"

"I—I'd have gone after Wolf and shot him dead. But I expected that I might die, too. Better that than living the way I have all these years."

"You're still a young woman, Clara. And still very attractive. You have a lot of life ahead."

"I hope so," she said. "Are you going after Wolf, then?"

"I am. He's already gotten the message from two different men, so he'll be looking over his shoulder from now on."

"What was your message?"

"Leave town or die," Slocum said.

She squeezed his hands then withdrew hers.

She looked long and earnestly at Slocum. She felt a quivering inside her stomach. He looked so strong and handsome up close and it was slightly unnerving to her. She hoped her feelings for him didn't show. But he had told her that she was attractive. That could mean anything. He probably didn't find her beautiful, but he seemed to like what she was made of, if nothing else.

She undid her bun and let her hair fall free and flowing over her back. There was a sheen to it in the soft glow from the lamp.

"You have pretty hair, Clara," he said as she brushed out the few minor tangles.

"Do you think I'm pretty?" she asked, and managed a wan smile.

"I think you're a very beautiful woman. Strong, honest, courageous, and with an inner strength that shows on your face. I like that in a woman. All those qualities, I mean."

"You're very kind."

"You've found yourself, Clara. You're not the same woman I saw in Fogarty's office. That was an actress playing a part. The real you is much more natural and beautiful."

"You seem to know more about me than I do myself," she said. "Maybe you know more about women than the average man."

He laughed. "I don't know about that. But I read people by looking at their faces and their actions. You have good qualities that have been hidden for a long time. No woman should have to go through what you did. Wolf's a heartless bastard to do what he did to you. He's a man who likes to see people suffer."

"Yes, he is. I hate him," she said. "I've hated him for a long, long time."

"Hate is a killer itself," he said. "It never gets you anywhere. You'll do well to give up your hate."

"How do I do that?" she asked.

"Find something or someone to love. That will take away the hate and give you back your senses."

She sighed and became thoughtful for a few seconds. What Slocum said made sense to her for some strange reason. Hate was an ugly thing. It had twisted her up inside and clouded her reason. It had blinded her to other possibilities in her life. Now she felt as if Slocum had drenched her in a cool gust of fresh air. Her mind was clearing and she could look not only back at her life, but ahead, to a better one.

"I like that idea," she said. "But Wolf is still there in my thoughts."

"He's no longer in your life, though, is he?"

She shook her head. "No, that's true. I've broken with him, whether he's dead or alive."

"That's part of your strength now, Clara."

She unbuttoned her coat and removed it. Slocum looked at her. Her shirt was unbuttoned and he could see part of her chest, the tiny brown freckles between her breasts. He felt a tug at his loins, a stirring in his groin.

Clara was more than an attractive woman, he thought. She had a grace that made her beautiful, desirable even.

She reached up to button her blouse.

"No, don't," he said.

"But the button's loose, John."

"Don't hide your beauty, Clara," he said with a smile.

She beamed back at him. "Why, John, I'm beginning to think you mean to seduce me."

"If I'm allowed," he said. "I'd like to seduce you."

She blushed and her face took on a rosy hue. She smiled coyly at him.

"You are starting to make my heart flutter," she said, her voice soft and low. "Flutter like crazy."

"The night is young," he said. "Like you. Young and sweet."

He stood up. Clara stood up, too. They came together, and he embraced her.

She tilted her head up, and he bent his neck to kiss her.

She was warm and willing. The kiss told it all. She quivered in his embrace, and he knew that she wanted him as much as he wanted her.

"Mmm," she moaned, and the kiss between them was long and lingering, full of promise, sweet with the taste.

He guided her to the bed as she unbuckled her gun belt.

"Now?" she said.

"If you want me."

"I want you, John. Oh, I want you so much."

"I want you, too, Clara."

He loosened his gun belt, rebuckled it, and hung it on the poster near his pillow. The two undressed as if they were burning up with the heat of their clothing.

She pulled the coverlet from the two pillows, and he gazed on her nakedness before he climbed into bed to lie beside her.

They embraced and clung to each other.

"Do you know how much I dreamed of this?" she asked.

"You've been cheated all these years," he said.

"I feel like a virgin. What Wolf did to me was not love, not loving. It was brutal and savage and . . ."

He put two fingers against her lips.

"Hush," he said. "That's all water over the dam. It's past. This is now, this moment, and we both have it."

"Yes, yes, we do," she said, and wrapped her arms around his neck. They kissed and then one of her hands squeezed the upper part of his leg. As if she were reassuring herself that he was real.

He stroked her breasts, gently rubbing his hand over their contours, as if he were a sculptor shaping a piece of soft clay.

She writhed with pleasure.

"Mm," she murmured. "Feels good. So good."

She bent her body to reach down and explore his groin. She grasped his tautening stalk and stroked it before her fingers closed around it. He grew harder with her touch.

"I—I've never done anything like this before," she whispered. "I feel so brazen all of a sudden."

"The woman you are is coming back out," he said. "This was what you were meant to do, Clara."

"Oh, that's so sweet of you to say that."

She squeezed his cock and he felt its veins engorge with blood. Like a jackknife, his prick opened fully and she stroked the smooth crown with the tip of her finger.

"You're such a man," she breathed.

He kissed both nipples, then slipped his hand between her

legs. She pulled them wider apart and he stroked her pussy, parting the lips. He probed inside with a finger and felt her juices flow, warm and wet as sun-warmed dew.

"Ah," she sighed, and he found her clitoris and stroked it until her entire body quivered and spasmed.

She cried out and squeezed his organ as if to pull him inside her.

He withdrew his finger from her warm wet cunt.

"Ready?" he asked.

"More than ready. Oh, John, thank you for this. I'm so grateful."

"I am, too, Clara. I want to pleasure you. I can't make up for all those years, but I can give you back some of what you missed."

"Oh, yes, you can, John. You can."

He mounted her and slid into her as she guided him through the portals of her sex, past the thatch of brown wiry hair and into the soft pudding of her pussy.

He plumbed her depths, and she responded with upward thrusts of her hips until they were in perfect rhythm. She undulated her hips as he pushed into her and he matched her every move with moves of his own.

Her body bucked and thrashed as she climaxed, and she swallowed the scream that issued unbidden from her throat.

Again and again she climaxed, and each time her spasms were more violent than before.

"Now, now," she purred as he increased the speed of his strokes. "I want your seed. All of it."

"I hope you're not in heat," he said half-jokingly.

"With you, I am," she said, and clung to him. Her fingernails dug into his back, but did not break the skin.

He felt the surge of energy, the rush of sperm that coursed like a mad flood up the pipe of his cock, and then he spilled his milk deep into her womb. He floated high above her on a white cloud of mindlessness that was fleeting and could never be recaptured.

Clara floated up there with him.

A blissful peacefulness filled her mind. Contentment flooded her being, and she clung to him in a state of pure rapture.

"We may never leave to go after Wolf," he said.

"I don't care. I no longer know who Wolf is. He's out of my life and forgotten."

But he knew that Wolf was not gone, and as long as he was in town, he was dangerous to both of them.

He wanted to lie with her and take her again.

But while Clara might have forgotten Wolf, he had not.

He steeled himself for what he had to do. He had to get up and get dressed and leave Clara or take her with him.

Either Wolf had left town by now, or he was waiting for Slocum to show up.

"I have to go," he said as he slid from the bed.

"I'm going with you," she said.

Slocum didn't say anything as he began to dress. He didn't want to encourage or discourage her. But in the back of his mind, he knew that she had a stake in seeing Wolf gone from her life and from Durango.

Maybe, he thought, it was foreordained.

But one way or another, Wolf had to disappear. From both of their lives.

That was Fate, he knew, as surely as if all of it were written in the stars.

24

Bert Loomis stretched his one serviceable leg as he sat by the window in Wolf's cabin. It had stiffened up on him, and he felt as if his circulation had shut down and the good leg—his right leg—was dying alongside the injured one. His left leg acted up regularly, with a sharp knifelike pain in the wound. He wished he could just drown himself in whiskey and sleep.

But Hobart and Wolf were banging around, stuffing supplies in their saddlebags, along with bullets and rifle cartridges. So far, Wolf had not told him what he was going to do. All he had heard were scraps of conversation between Hobart and Wolf that he could not decipher, as if they were talking in another tongue or in some kind of gibberish code.

He was growing angrier by the minute.

Finally, the two men came into the front room, with saddlebags slung over their shoulders.

"We're leavin'," Wolf said to Loomis.

"Where you goin', boss?"

"For a ride."

"This time of night?"

"You stay put, Bert. No tellin' who might show up."

"What do I do if that Slocum feller comes around?"

"Shoot him," Wolf said.

Hobart laughed.

"What are you laughin' at, Cornelius?" Loomis said with a whining underline to Hobart's given name.

"I told you not to call me that, Bert," Hobart said. He hated his first name and almost never used it. And he hated to be called "Hobie." Some who had called him that had broken jaws that he'd delivered free of charge.

"We might be back, Bert," Wolf said. "All depends."

"On what?" Loomis asked.

"If we run into Slocum, we'll drop him and then it's business as usual."

"I hope you run into him," Loomis said.

Hobart and Wolf left the cabin and walked the few blocks to the stables, past all the little Mexican stores, cantinas, and cafés. They passed the yard where the Mexicans stored their carts and wagons, a few doors from the livery stables, which was the largest in town, and the most accessible.

Palacio de Caballos stood in a large tract nestled against a towering mountain at the back, so its large corral only had to be fenced on three sides.

It was dark on the street, but there were lanterns burning inside the stable, which was one of the largest buildings in town, complete with a hay loft, a tack room, and a blacksmith's shop off to the side in another structure.

Benito Aguilar was on duty. He was not the owner, but he groomed and fed the horses, and acted as night watchman. The stables were owned by Eladio Salazar, a tough, trail-wise Mexican from Sonora who had been one of the earliest settlers in Durango. A white-haired, bearded man, he knew horses and cattle like he knew the back of his hand.

"Mr. Wolf," Benito said when Hobart and Wolf walked down the stalls toward one that Aguilar was cleaning with a pitchfork and shovel. He had a wheelbarrow parked outside the stall and a lantern hanging on a twenty-penny nail to give him light. "You come to visit your horse?"

"I'm going to saddle up, Benny," Wolf said. "Hobart wants his horse, too."

"Yes, I will show you where they are and open the tack room for you to get your saddles."

Benito left the stall and led them to the tack room. He took out a ring of keys and unlocked the padlock. He lit a lantern and hung it on a wire loop that was attached to the ceiling.

Wolf and Hobart set down their saddlebags a few feet apart outside the tack room.

"Your horses are in the small corral," Aguilar said. "I will get them for you." He took two rope halters from the wall and left the two men to find their saddles and bridles.

"Smells like horseshit in here," Hobart said.

"Just be glad it ain't sheep dip," Wolf cracked back.

Hobart chuckled as he found his saddle with the rifle scabbard attached. He lugged it outside and lay it on its side. Then he found his bridle on a dowel set into the wall along with several others. Wolf lugged his saddle out, along with his bridle, and lay them next to Hobart's.

Benito returned in a few moments. He led two horses into the livery, both prancing and eager to see their masters. Both horses whickered when they saw their owners. Some of the horses inside the stalls neighed. There was the pungent aroma of hay and horse manure inside the livery, and flies buzzed here and there as they flew up from piles of fresh offal.

"I will saddle your horses," Benito said to Wolf. "You have the blankets?"

"Couldn't find 'em," Wolf said.

"I know where they are," Benito said. He went into the tack room and came out with two saddle blankets, both with different patterns woven into the wool. He laid them on the right saddles as he picked up the two bridles.

Wolf and Hobart watched as Aguilar slipped off the halters from their horses and replaced them with their bridles. Wolf's horse was a dappled gray and Hobart's was a paint, both stocky and only fourteen or fifteen hands high, what the cowboys called cow ponies, with dubious bloodlines.

"Benny, give us a couple of hatfuls of grain in a feed sack, will you?"

"Coming right up," Benito said.

He went into another room, which housed barrels of corn and oats and bins of alfalfa and other grasses. He emerged with a flour sack of corn and oats, which he handed to Hobart. Hobart stuffed the sack into one of his saddlebags.

Wolf and Hobart both checked their cinches, then laid on their saddlebags and cinched them to their saddles.

"You will come back, Mr. Wolf?" Benito asked.

"Maybe," Wolf said. "Could be a very short ride, or a very long one."

Benito laughed, not because he understood, but because he didn't. He just did not want to look stupid in front of these two men.

Wolf and Hobart slid their rifles into their separate scabbards, gave one last tug on the single cinches of their saddles, and led their horses from the stables.

"Good night, Mr. Wolf," Benito called after them.

"Night," Wolf said and seated his hat tighter on his head.

Outside, the two men mounted their horses.

"Where to, boss?" Hobart asked.

"Let's hitch up at the saloon. Have one for the road."

"I'm all for that," Hobart said.

They rode the few blocks to the saloon and dismounted, tied their reins to one of the hitch rails out front, and walked into the saloon.

They went straight to the bar as Wolf glanced at the patrons. The usual crowd was there—Mexicans who worked the mines or hauled equipment to the various claims; a few drifters, some down on their luck with sad faces; miners and prospectors; and an old lady or two with their fans and cheap rings, enlarged bosoms, and drab dresses looking for any man who would buy them a drink and maybe take them to bed after the saloon closed.

Joe came up to where the two men sat at the end of the bar.

"Back again. What'll it be, gents?" he asked.

"Whiskey," Wolf said. "The good stuff, not that rotgut you serve those swine lining the bar."

Joe laughed uncomfortably.

"You know, Wolf, that I only serve you our best brand of ninety-proof."

"Yeah, yeah," Wolf said. "Watered down sometimes."

"Not by me," Joe said.

"I'll have rye," Hobart said. "Two fingers."

"Rye it is," Joe said, and drifted away to fetch glasses and bottles.

Wolf looked at the saloon girls who sat at the tables with their skimpy dresses and a lot of leg showing, encased in black mesh. But he was looking for someone else and he spotted her, finally, when she arose from one of the far tables at the very back of the large room.

Amy Sullivan had been talking to some friends, the man and the woman who owned the dry goods store in town. They were an older couple who liked hard cider before they toddled off to their home and bed.

She had seen Wolf and Hobart come in, with their heavy jackets on, and walk to the bar. Which was unusual. Wolf almost never sat at the bar. He always took a table where he could watch who came in and who went out. That was curious enough, but the men were dressed as if they were leaving town.

She wondered if Slocum's message had sunk into Wolf's brain enough to make him worry about living to see another sunrise in Durango.

She walked slowly across the room and came up to where the two men were sitting, their hands on the bar, their fingers intertwined.

"Amy," Wolf said. "Hello again."

"Wolf. Surprised you're here at the bar. Are you not going to stay long?"

She tried to hide her disgust of the man. She ignored Hobart completely.

"No, we won't be here long. Just in for a nightcap, you might say."

"Well, enjoy yourself," she said and started to walk away.

Wolf swiveled around on his stool and grabbed her arm.

"Oh, don't rush off," he said to her. "I got something to show you."

"Let loose of my arm," she said, a cold hard tone to her voice.

Wolf let her go. He smiled at her and she couldn't help thinking how much his name fitted him. His smile was like that of a savage wolf, fangs and all.

"Sorry," he said. "Just didn't want you to leave just yet."

Joe brought their glasses and two bottles. He poured the rye and the whiskey, and Wolf dug into his pocket and laid some bills on the bar top.

"Thanks, Wolf," Joe said. "You've got change coming."

"Keep it, Joe," Wolf said, "and take the bottles back where you got 'em."

"Just one drink for both of you?" Joe said.

"Just one," Wolf said.

Joe picked up the bottles and walked down the bar to put them back on the shelf against the wall.

Amy stood there, a scowl on her face. "What's on your mind, Wolf?" she asked.

"I brought you something, Miss Amy," he said. "I got it outside because I didn't want a lot of people in here gawking at it."

"I don't want any gifts from you," she said, trying to put some politeness into her voice.

"The gift is not from me," Wolf said.

"Not from you? Who's it from?" Amy was genuinely puzzled.

"It's supposed to be a surprise, so I can't rightly tell you. You have to see it for yourself."

"I can't imagine. What's the gift?"

"Can't tell you that either, Miss Any," Wolf said. "But I got it and I promised this person to deliver it to you before I leave town."

"Oh, you're leaving Durango?" Amy studied his face to see if he really meant what he had said. She saw no deception there.

"Yep. Soon as I down this here drink," Wolf said.

He turned from her and upended the glass of whiskey into his mouth. Hobart drank his rye down in a single gulp. He was as puzzled as Amy was because Wolf had not said anything to him and he didn't know what kind of surprise he had for Amy.

Wolf swiped his sleeve across his mouth and slid from the stool.

"Hobart, you go on out and wait for me and Miss Amy. We'll be along right after you."

Amy backed a step away from Wolf as Hobart slid off his stool and marched to the door like an obedient soldier.

"I—I don't know, Wolf," she said as the batwings swung

until they stopped in the wake of Hobart's exit. "I'm not expecting anything from anyone and certainly not a surprise, like you say it is."

"Well, you'll be surprised, Miss Amy."

"Is it from someone I know?"

"Oh, yes, you know her."

"It's a she, then."

"That much I can tell you," he said, and that warm, disarming smile returned to his face.

"Well, I just don't know what to say," she said.

"No need to say anything. Come on with me. It won't take but a minute and then I can be on my way."

"Where you going?" she asked.

"Pagosa Springs," he said quickly, without hesitation.

"Oh."

He got off his stool and held out his arm for her to take it. She ignored the offering. So Wolf walked toward the door, a slow step at a time.

Curious, Amy walked with him.

She saw the horses at the hitch rail. Hobart sat on his paint and he held the reins of the dappled gray in his hand for Wolf.

"Where's the surprise?" she asked.

"Over here, at the corner of the saloon," he said. He pointed to a dark place beyond one of the front windows.

"I don't see anything," she said.

"Just walk on over there and you'll see it," he said.

Reluctantly, Amy walked past the window to the corner of the building. She stared at the ground and started to peer around the corner when she heard footsteps behind her.

She turned, suddenly afraid, and saw Wolf advancing toward her, almost on tiptoe. Quietly.

He jerked his pistol from its holster.

"Here's your surprise, you bitch," he said. "This is for Jimmy John and a preview of what's going to happen to that bastard, Slocum."

Amy opened her mouth to scream, but she heard the click of the hammer as Wolf cocked it, and she froze.

Wolf squeezed the trigger as he pointed the barrel straight at the middle of her forehead a half foot away from her.

The explosion split the silence of the night.

A round hole appeared in Amy's forehead and she crumpled like a sad thrown-away doll to the ground.

Wolf holstered his pistol and dashed to his horse.

He climbed into the saddle and grabbed his reins from Hobart.

"Let's light shuck, Hobart," Wolf said and turned his horse away from the hitch rail.

"Holy Christ," Hobart said. "I didn't expect you to shoot down no woman, boss," Hobart said as they trotted away from the saloon.

"She's the one who told Slocum that Jimmy John was out back. Got him killed. I hate a slut like that."

"I guess you purely do," Hobart said.

They put their horses into a gallop and disappeared up the street as patrons in the saloon rushed out through the batwing doors to see what had happened outside.

A woman screamed.

Amy lay dead in a pool of blood, her eyes fixed on eternity, unseeing, glassy as smoked crystal marbles.

Somewhere, up on the mountain, a wolf howled long and mournful and men gasped at the sight of the beautiful woman lying there dead, a hole in her forehead.

And most of those who stood there knew just who had killed Amy.

Wolf.

25

There was no one in the lobby of the hotel when Slocum and Clara stopped to leave his key at the clerk's counter. A sign on the counter said the clerk was out for thirty minutes, with no explanation.

Slocum's saddlebags were slung over his left shoulder, along with a wooden canteen. Before he left the room, he had hidden his belly gun at his waist behind his belt buckle, and he carried his Winchester in his left hand. He felt weighted down on one side, and the only counterbalance was his hotel key.

There was a slot where room keys could be dropped so that they would not lie on the counter for anyone to take. Slocum dropped his key through the slot. He heard it strike other keys.

"This is one of the hotels where you should sleep with a gun close by your bed," Slocum said.

"It's not the Ritz," Clara said.

They walked outside and looked up at the stars, the satin black sky with the Milky Way a sprawl of sparkling jewels, the moon not yet risen.

Slocum sniffed. He reeked of Clara's musk and it was a satisfying aroma. She was some woman, he thought. Wasted for all those years. Deprived of affection and loving. It was a dirty shame.

"You keep your horse at the livery, Clara?" Slocum asked.

She nodded. "I try to see her almost every day. A bay mare

141

I call Rose, only because the name seems to fit her. She's a dark bay with three white stockings."

"Let's saddle up and ride over to Wolf's. See if he wants some company."

"If he's there, he'll have a man or two watching for you," she said.

"Are you a good shot with that two-dollar pistol?" Slocum asked.

"It cost more than two dollars, John. And yes, I'm a good shot. With either pistol or rifle."

"Ever kill a man? Or a woman?" he asked.

Clara shook her head. "Not yet."

"Big game?"

"I've shot deer and elk. I've got good eyes."

"Who taught you to shoot?" he asked.

"Wolf," she said with a wry smile on her lips. "But he doesn't know I have this pistol. And he never gave me a gun of my own."

"Do you know why?"

"I'm sure he doesn't want me to use a gun on him," she said. "I bought the pistol from a passing drummer we ran into when we were outrunning a posse in Kansas. Wolf was off shooting at rattlesnakes and prairie chickens, and I had saved money from my allowance. I paid the drummer five dollars and fifty cents for that pistol, and I practiced shooting it every time Wolf wasn't around. When I bought groceries for the gang, I bought cartridges for my Smith & Wesson."

"Smart woman," he said. Then he hitched his belt and straightened his holster. "Let's go saddle up and pay Wolf a visit," he said.

Just then, they both heard a resounding explosion. A gunshot that rattled the windows of the hotel.

It came from the saloon.

Both Slocum and Clara turned at the sound of the shot and stared down the street where the saloon's windows sprayed a dull yellow light onto the dirt street.

Slocum saw a man on horseback and another horse, saddled, sidling back and forth at the end of the reins in the mounted man's hands.

Seconds later, a man dashed out of the shadows and hauled

himself up into the saddle of the unmanned horse. They turned and trotted up the street toward them. The horses broke into a gallop and the two men passed by.

"That's Wolf," Clara gasped.

"Who's with him?" Slocum asked.

"Looked like Hobart. Yes, it was Hobart, I'm sure."

They both ran toward the saloon. They saw the people emerging from it and huddle up at one corner. They reached the edge of the crowd.

"Wait here," Slocum said, and elbowed his way through the small mob. They were all looking downward.

Then Slocum broke through the bar patrons and saw what they were looking at on the ground. He recognized the distinctive dress first. Then he saw her face, which was starting to sag and change shape.

He saw Amy Sullivan lying dead, a bullet hole in her forehead. He pushed the people away and stooped over to look at her. There was brain matter in her hair at the back of her head. A dark pool was beneath her head. Her eyes were open and glazed. He saw that much, even in the hazy light from the saloon.

He cursed under his breath and made his way back through the pushing crowd of gawkers.

Clara's face was drawn when he took her by the arm and led her away from the saloon.

"Somebody dead?" she asked.

"Yes," Slocum said. "The woman who was in charge of the girls in the saloon."

"Amy?"

"Yes, Amy. You knew her?"

"I spoke to her a few times. She was nice. Is—is she dead, really?"

"Really. Shot in the forehead."

Clara stifled a sob.

"Wolf," she breathed, and then she was running with Slocum toward the livery stable. They had to cut between buildings for several blocks.

By the time they reached the livery stable, she was out of breath. And she was stunned that a pretty woman like Amy Sullivan had been shot dead. Even if Wolf had done it.

"Why would he shoot that woman?" Clara asked as they entered the lantern-lit stables with its musky smell and the sounds of horses moving and eating in their stalls.

Benito emerged from a stall and turned over a shovel to spill horse feces into a wheelbarrow. He looked toward them.

"Ah, you have come to see your horse, Mr. Slocum," Benito said as Slocum strode into the cone of yellowish lantern light. "And you bring Miss Morgan with you."

"Fetch our horses, Benito, and we're in a hurry," he said.

"The tack room is still open and you can see to get your saddles, bridles, and blankets," he said. "Your horses are right here. I will get them."

As Slocum and Clara walked to the tack room, Slocum leaned toward her and whispered an answer to her question.

"Amy died because she helped me," he said. "I'll tell you all about it later."

Slocum tried to quell the grief he felt for Amy. To see such a vibrant, giving woman lying dead on a dirty street infused him with an overwhelming sadness. And now, with Clara's scent all over his body, he felt Amy's tragic death even more acutely. She died, he knew, with his own scent on her, and perhaps his seed still inside her. In the shadow of his grief was a boiling anger, a hatred so deep and so strong it threatened to cloud his judgment.

He wanted to kill Wolf now. Which went against his grain. For his warning to Wolf had been that if he left town, he would live.

But he would break that promise.

Wolf did not deserve to live another day. He had brutally murdered a fine young woman, a beautiful woman, and that was a sin none could forgive.

As he waited for Ferro to be brought to him, Slocum felt as if he were in some kind of limbo, a place between heaven and hell, a no-man's-land where all was desolate and barren, a wasteland on which only he stood, alone with his black thoughts and his growing hatred for a man he had never met, an evil that was like a cancer on the earth.

This, he knew, was a dangerous place to be. For in his anger, there was a blindness, too, a wall against reality. Wolf was a dangerous man, and to hunt him down and kill him would take all of his concentration, all of his will, and all of his clarity of mind and thinking.

His anger could dull his senses, slow his gun hand down, block his acute and accurate vision so that he could not beat Wolf, but would likely be defeated by him.

Clara tugged on his arm as if he had fallen asleep while standing up.

"Our horses, John," she said. "Benny has our horses."

He turned toward her as if he had just been jolted out of a deep slumber.

But he knew where he had been. He had been at Wolf's throat, ripping it out with his bare hands and cursing the man, damning him to an eternal hell where fires lapped at his flesh and consumed him for all eternity.

"Yeah," he said. "I was just thinking."

"About Wolf," she said.

"Partly," he replied, and saw Ferro bob his head and stamp the ground with his right hoof.

And there was Clara's bay mare, alongside his tall black horse, looking at her with wide brown eyes and nickering softly.

They saddled the horses as Benito watched.

"Did Wolf say where he was going?" Slocum asked Aguilar.

"No. He just asked for grain. I gave him two quarts."

Slocum thought about that. A hatful for each horse, Wolf's and Hobart's. No more than a day's ride from town.

Slocum and Clara got grain from Benito and walked the horses outside the stables.

Slocum waved to Benito as he mounted Ferro, checked his rifle to see that it was securely seated in its scabbard.

"I've got jerky and hardtack in my saddlebags if you get hungry," he said to Clara.

"Right now, I'm on fire inside," she said. "I couldn't think about eating anything."

"Just to let you know I won't let you starve, Clara."

She laughed.

"Do you know where Wolf is going?" she asked. "Maybe up in the mountains where he can lie in wait and bush-whack us?"

"I don't think he's going to do that," Slocum said.

"Where, then?"

"My guess is that he's headed for Pagosa Springs. So we ride east on the road and keep our eyes peeled in case he's waiting to jump anybody who's chasing him."

"Good guess," she said. "Wolf might want to hole up in a town. A small town like Pagosa Springs."

"We won't hurry this," Slocum said. "He and Hobart will run their horses until they're winded and then slow down. They'll watch their back trail. The more time we give him, the more sure of himself he'll get. He'll let his guard down some maybe, and won't be expecting me or a posse."

"He's very good at outrunning posses," she said.

"We'll see how good he is," Slocum said.

They rode through the nearly empty spaces between houses and cabins and up the main street into the maw of a canyon that was as dark as pitch.

Every so often, Slocum halted his horse and held out an arm to stop Clara. Then he sat his horse and listened for any alien sound.

Clara grew more confident that Slocum knew what he was doing as she watched his behavior on the trail of Wolf and Hobart.

She felt safe with him, as she had never felt with Wolf or any of his men. And she was still glowing from the lovemaking that had renewed her vigor and rejuvenated her womanhood. Slocum had made her feel like a real person again, a dead flower that had suddenly sprung to life under the warming waters of love.

They rode up the dark canyon above and to the east of Durango. They heard the wolves howl from various locations, and when they stopped, they could hear deer and elk up in the timber, the hundreds of sounds from small animals foraging for food in the night. And they saw a silent owl float across the road, its wings spread wide and softly beating the dark air.

Somewhere, ahead of them, was the man they both hated.

The man they both wanted to kill.

Wolf Steiner.

A plague upon the earth, a monster, a murderer.

And both of them wanted him dead for different reasons.

26

Some forty minutes after Amy was shot and killed, Constable Abner Hellinger and his deputy, Elmer Craig, arrived at the saloon to view the body and question witnesses.

Someone had placed a blue bandanna over Amy's face—out of respect, or perhaps to hide the hideous sight from onlookers. Hellinger removed the bandanna and gazed at the corpse dressed in the colors of the Mexican flag. He shook his head.

"Pity," he grunted. "Such a beautiful lady, taken from this life long before her time."

"I didn't know her real well, but she was always nice," Craig said.

"Well, Elmer, get some men and take her body over to Enrique's."

Enrique Monsanto was the local undertaker and proprietor of Puerto de Cielo Funeral Parlor.

"Enrique's runnin' out of room over yonder," Elmer said.

"Get two men from the saloon. I got to ask some questions. Shake a leg."

Elmer left to go into the saloon. The constable replaced the bandanna over Amy's face and walked around the body as if looking for clues. There was nothing there to draw his attention. He walked into the saloon and leaned over the bar, twiching a finger at Joe to come and talk to him.

Joe walked to the end of the bar where Hellinger stood,

wiping his hands with a bar towel. There was a steady hum of conversation in the large room as people spoke of the killing. The saloon girls were still dabbing at their faces as fresh tears flowed from their mascara-daubed eyes.

"Joe, what do you know about that gal gettin' shot?" Hellinger asked.

"All I know is that Wolf and Hobart come in here for drinks. Amy come over and chewed the fat with 'em for a minute or two. Next thing I see is Hobart walkin' out and then, maybe a minute later, Wolf, him, and Amy go outside together. Then I heard a shot, and next thing I know, Wolf and Hobart are ridin' up the street. When I got out there, Amy was ringed by a crowd and I saw that she was plumb dead. A sorry sight."

"So you think what?"

"I think Wolf shot her dead, that's what."

Joe set the towel in front of him on the bar. He had tears in his eyes.

"That all?" Hellinger asked.

"She was one fine woman, Abner. A damned shame. I hope Wolf rots in hell."

"Any idea why he would shoot that woman? Kill her in cold blood like that?"

Joe shook his head. "I can't imagine why anyone would want to kill Amy. But I saw her talkin' to that feller who wears black earlier in the evenin'."

"Slocum?"

"That's the feller. Maybe that had something to do with why Wolf killed Amy."

"Umm. Maybe. Thanks, Joe."

Out of the corner of his eye, he saw Elmer take two men with him out the front door and onto the street. Two hard-rock miners who could easily tote a woman of Amy's size over to Enrique's. He tapped the bar and left Joe standing there. Joe wiped his eyes with a corner of the bar towel. Every person in the saloon watched the constable walk through the batwing doors and then the talk rose up again and filled the room with spoken words, speculative opinions.

When he got outside, Hellinger saw the two men lift Amy's body. One held her by the feet, the other by the shoulders. The one they called Geezer had removed the bandanna and it was hanging loose from one of his back pockets. The other man, holding her shoulders, he knew as Chunk. He did not know their real names.

He spoke to Craig, who was about to lead the men the two blocks to the funeral home.

"When you finish up at Enrique's, Elmer, come on by the office. We got some work to do."

"Sure, thing, boss," Elmer said.

Hellinger lit the lamp on his desk. He had piles of papers, including a notarized deposition from Lou Darvin, attesting to the facts surrounding the murder of Jasper Nichols. And he had gotten a statement from Stacey Clemson earlier that evening about the murder of Jasper's brother, Wilbur. While she hadn't actually killed Wilbur, she was certainly an accomplice. He also had warrants for Wolf, Hobart, and others of his gang, most of whom were now dead. One man he could arrest immediately, and for whom he had a warrant, was Bert Loomis.

But he also had a search warrant for Abel Fogarty, which Judge George Carroway had signed. Fogarty was a suspect in the forgeries of mining claims, all of which were transferred to one Wolfgang Steiner.

Stacey had been very helpful, and he thought she might get off any serious charges by becoming a witness against Wolf, Fogarty, and the whole rotten bunch.

These cases were the most Hellinger had ever handled, and while he felt a sense of pride that he had done his job well, he was also weary from the amount of evidence he'd gathered and had to present to the prosecuting attorney who would appear before Judge Carroway.

When Elmer walked into his office, Hellinger had all the papers he needed stuffed in his coat pocket. There were also a half-dozen pairs of handcuffs in the middle of his desk.

"What are them for?" Elmer asked.

"Criminals," Hellinger said. "Grab as many as you can and stuff 'em in your pockets and I'll tote the rest."

"Golly," Elmer said and scooped up four pairs of handcuffs. "We're goin' to need a wagon. Maybe a Black Mariah."

Hellinger chuckled.

"Ever hear of a chain gang, Elmer? We just march 'em back to jail in single file, guns at their backs."

"I guess that would work—if we can catch 'em."

The two set out for Wolf's cabin. That would be Hellinger's first stop and the next one could wait until morning, if necessary.

Bert Loomis saw them coming.

He did not know who it was at first. But he saw two men cross the street and head straight for him. He slid his chair away from the window so that he could lean over and look out. He grabbed the butt of his pistol.

When the men got close, he recognized Constable Hellinger.

"What the hell . . ." he mumbled to himself.

Then there was a knock on the door. Loomis rose to open it. He felt a stabbing pain in his leg as he limped to the door and unlatched it.

"Loomis?" Hellinger said.

"Yeah. Wolf's not here."

"I didn't come to see Wolf. I know he left town. I've got a warrant for your arrest."

Hellinger pushed the door open. He and Elmer came in. Loomis stepped aside.

"What for?" Loomis asked.

Hellinger reached over and pulled Loomis's pistol from its holster. He handed the gun to Elmer.

"Attempted murder."

"I didn't attempt no murder," Loomis said, his anger visible on his suddenly florid face.

"Jasper Nichols," Hellinger said. "I have a witness. Hold out your hands."

Loomis stiffened. He did not stick out his hands, but backed away from the constable and his deputy.

"You got it wrong, Constable. I was just there. I never even drawed my gun."

"You were close enough. You're going to jail, Loomis. Now stick out your hands or I'll clobber you with the butt of my pistol."

Reluctantly, Loomis put his arms out.

Hellinger took a pair of cuffs from his pocket and handed them to Craig.

Elmer put the handcuffs around Loomis's wrists and shut them tight. So tight that Loomis winced when they clicked shut.

"Out," Hillinger said, and shoved Loomis into the doorway.

"This is all wrong," Loomis said. "I ain't guilty of nothin'."

"Shut up, Loomis," Hellinger said and closed the door.

"What about Wolf? And Hobart? You goin' to arrest them, too?"

"That's none of your business. Now shut up once and for all, or I'll sure as hell give you a bloody lip."

"Shit," Loomis said.

Hellinger whacked him on the back and Loomis said no more.

The constable and his deputy marched their prisoner to the jail. There were only two cells. Both were empty. They put Loomis in one of them and locked the iron door with the heavy bars. He limped to a cot and sat down, holding his leg near the wound.

Craig held a lantern high to give them light.

"Can I talk now?" Loomis asked.

"If you got anything to say. You're not innocent, so don't give me no more of that guff."

"I know a lot, Constable. About Wolf and his schemes. It was him what ordered us to kill that kid at the freight office. You make it light on me and I'll talk plenty about what's been goin' on."

"I'm right sure you'd do that, Loomis," Hellinger said. "Birds like you always sing when they're put in a cage. I ain't makin' no promise, but if you can give the prosecutin' attorney a rundown on your gang, he might go easy on you."

"And I need a sawbones," Loomis said. "That feller Slocum put a bullet through my leg."

"Not tonight," Hellinger said. "Maybe in the mornin'. You sleep tight, boy."

"Don't I get nothin'? No water, no grub?"

"Nothin'. There's a chamber pot under your bunk and a wad of paper."

Loomis mumbled a string of curses.

Hellinger and Craig walked back into the office, plunging the jail cell into darkness. They heard the creak of the old cot as Loomis lay down.

Craig closed the door.

"Well, that's that," he said. "We goin' to arrest anybody else tonight?"

"No. In the morning, we'll go over to the claims office and pay Mr. Fogarty a visit. You get some sleep."

"Enrique was pretty durned mad when we brought Amy in. Said he was plumb full and would have to hire another carpenter."

"He'll get over it. City will pay him something for his troubles and he'll get a coroner's fee."

"A lot of killin' lately," Craig said.

He set the lantern down on a table near the desk, where a lamp still flickered.

"I'm counting on a couple more," Hellinger said.

"Huh? Who?"

"Unless I miss my guess, I'd say Slocum is hot on Wolf's trail right now. I expect he won't come back empty-handed. He'll be leading two horses with dead bodies on them. Then Enrique will have plenty to holler about."

"Jesus," Craig said.

He left the office, shaking his head.

Hellinger sat at his desk and rubbed his chin, the short hairs of a stubble growing from his flesh.

Slocum, he thought. He did not know for sure if Slocum had chased after Wolf, but he would find out in the morning. There was something about that man that bothered him. Why was he at the center of all the recent murders and shootings? He had no stake in Durango. He had ridden in here only to deliver some horses, and yet he'd stayed to clean up the town. He was like some knight of old, and Hellinger would bet money that Slocum knew Amy Sullivan and somehow Wolf had put it all together and killed her because of Slocum. Otherwise, her murder didn't make sense.

Yes, he would bet that Slocum knew more about Amy's murder than anybody else did, including himself.

Where did a man like Slocum come from anyway? he wondered.

Maybe out of nowhere.

And back into nowhere once he had finished what Fate had called upon him to do.

Hellinger put out the lantern flame and blew out the lamp on his desk. He made his way to the door in darkness and let himself out. He locked the door and walked to his home a pair of blocks away, weary, but somehow elated.

Maybe, he thought, he should deputize Slocum and put him on permanent.

But in his heart he knew that a man like Slocum never put down roots. He was a drifter, and maybe, if he looked hard and long enough, a drifter with a price on his head.

It was, somehow, a comforting thought.

Slocum might be a wanted man who was now on the right side of the law.

27

Wolf and Hobart rode along a narrow trail through a steep dark canyon that seemed endless. The only smattering of light came from the Animas River with its star-sprinkled waves and murky waters that swallowed most of the distant lights in the sky.

The temperature dropped as a cold wind blew through the chimney of the canyon. The wind scorched their faces and scoured their skin as if made of rough sandpaper. The men bent over their saddle horns to allow their hat brims to deflect some of the wind away from their faces. But the cold fingers pried through their jackets. They shivered in the harsh chill that seemed to penetrate into their bones.

"Damned wind," Hobart said.

"It's a bitch willy," Wolf said. "It's like a damned tunnel through an iceberg."

"Hard as hell to see anything, too," Hobart said.

"The horses will find their way out of here. No need to look at the road. I don't even know if we're on the road," Wolf said. "If the river wasn't there, I'd think we were lost."

"Maybe we ought to head for the timber and build a lean-to out of this damned wind," Hobart said.

"The horses would have to scale sheer rock to get to any timber," Wolf grumbled.

His anger rose in counterpoint to the cold. He felt as if he had been chased out of a warm cabin by a phantom dressed in black, a man he did not know, but who had decimated his men like a one-man army. The bastard. Maybe, he thought, he should have stayed and faced the man. After all, he was no slouch with a pistol and he still had Hobart to back him.

No use in crying over spilled milk, Wolf thought. He couldn't go back to Durango right now. He was frozen stiff from the bitter cold and couldn't draw his pistol if he had to. So Slocum had won that round. He would not win the next. If the man managed to track them to Pagosa Springs, he and Hobart would be warm by then and ready to shoot him down if he showed his face.

That thought helped to ward off the cold that seeped through his flesh and curdled his bones. There was still money for the taking in Durango, and as soon as the weather warmed up, he meant to go back and rake in his share of the wealth.

"I—I'm freezin' to death, Wolf," Hobart said as the canyon seemed to darken and the wind blow harder.

"Quit your damned bellyachin', Hobart. Just grit your teeth and keep on goin'."

The horses blew frosty vapor from their rubbery nostrils, and Wolf could see his own breath as it streamed from his mouth in a mist.

"Shit, we're never goin' to get out of this canyon," Hobart complained. "All I see ahead is more rock, more hellish cliffs."

"There's an end to everything," Wolf said and felt the gelid air burn his lungs when he drew in oxygen.

He hated Hobart's whining. It was a sign of weakness. Wolf couldn't stand weakness in a man or a woman. His brother had been weak, and so was Clara. He hated her more than he hated anyone. He hated her for choosing Hans over him so long ago, and hated her for having kids he didn't want, and even hated her for kowtowing to him over the years. Scared of her own shadow. You could not trust a weakling, he thought. Sooner or later a weakling would buckle under pressure. Someone like that could let you down when the going was rough.

Hobart had been a good man, but he, too, was turning into a spineless weakling over a little cold weather. What would happen to him when he faced the barrel of a Colt .45? Would his teeth chatter and his knees turn to jelly when faced with a man like Slocum?

Wolf ground his teeth to keep them from clacking together. Yes, it was damned cold, but he wouldn't give Hobart the satisfaction of knowing that he, too, was freezing, that his body seemed lifeless in the saddle.

After what seemed like hours, the canyon began to widen. The sheer bluffs on either side receded, and the river was a ribbon of spangles shimmering in the light of the risen moon. The road climbed at a grade that seemed to rise slowly above the pit they had been in for the past two hours.

He saw Hobart tilt his head and look upward at the moon, then shrug back down and huddle over his pommel like a beggar.

Wolf shook his body to warm it up. That didn't work. The chill was still there, deep in every fiber of his body, in his goose-pimpled arms, the shiver steady and uncontrollable as it coursed up and down his frame from his numb feet to his forehead.

Another half hour of steady plodding brought them to a rise, and then they were out of the canyon and away from the harsh wind. It was still very cold, but at least their coats were some protection. Wolf flapped one arm against his side, then the other. His fingers were wooden, and he flexed them to bring back circulation to their tips.

Suddenly, Hobart looked up ahead and raised his left hand to signal Wolf, who rode behind him in single file.

"There's somethin' up ahead yonder," Hobart said as he turned to look back at Wolf.

Wolf stood up in the stirrups and saw a shadowy blob off to the side of the road. It seemed to be moving just a little. "What is it?" he asked.

"Dunno," Hobart answered. He looked ahead once more and thought he saw a man. He pulled his rifle from its scabbard with a clumsy hand that had no feeling in it.

Wolf lifted his coat on the right side and put his hand on his pistol. He could barely feel the outline of his pistol grip. He patted his fingers against the wood and felt no sensation at all.

As they got closer, Hobart made out the silhouette of a horse.

Then, a few seconds later, he saw a man on foot beside it. He brought his rifle up and laid it across the pommel.

The man on the ground waved both arms in a wigwag fashion.

Wolf saw it, too, as he rode alongside Hobart.

"That's Jessup," Wolf said.

"Damned if it ain't," Hobart agreed.

They rode up on Tom Jessup, but could barely see his face. He had a bandanna tied under his chin, the top of it beneath his crumpled felt hat.

"Jesus, Hobart, am I glad as hell to see you," Jessup said.

"What're you doin' here, Tom?" Hobart asked Wolf's errand boy.

"Horse stepped in a hole and he's gone lame on me."

"The hell you say."

"Can't feel no broken bones, but this is as far as I've got."

"I can see that," Wolf said.

"Let's have a look," Hobart said.

He dismounted and let his reins fall free. His horse stood there, blowing clouds of mist through its nostrils.

Wolf looked at Jessup's horse. Its head was drooping and its tail hung straight. Its left hoof was cocked above the ground as it stood on three legs.

Hobart squatted down as Jessup walked around to stand near him.

"Happened about a quarter mile back," Jessup said. "We was goin' along just fine then Willie here stumbled and come up lame. I felt his hock. He winced ever' time I touched it, so I don't know if there's a bone broke in his ankle or not."

Hobart touched the bottom of Willie's hoof and pushed upward gently. The horse let out a whinny of pain and stepped aside and away from him on three legs.

"He's pained, that's for sure," Hobart said. "What'd you do, boy, step in a gopher hole?" He reached up and patted the horse's neck. Willie tossed its head.

"I'd say he stuck his leg in some kind of a hole," Hobart said. "Might have sprained his ankle or, worse, broke a little bone somewhere inside."

"I'm stuck here, that's for sure," Jessup said.

"Shoot the horse," Wolf called down from his high perch.

"Oh no, not Willie," Jessup said.

"You can walk him to the Springs, then," Wolf said. "Might take you a day or two."

Jessup stood up and rubbed his forehead with a gloved hand.

"If nothin's broke," Tom said, "he might heal up pretty quick. How far is to the Springs?"

"I don't know," Wolf said. "A far piece."

"Shit," Jessup said.

Hobart took off his glove and with a numb finger traced a line down Willie's ankle until the horse flinched. "There," he said.

"What?" Jessup asked.

"It's high above the ankle. Maybe an inch or two. Not good."

"What do you mean?" Tom asked.

"I mean, I think he's got a bone broke above his ankle. It ain't somethin' that will cure right off."

"Damn," Jessup exclaimed.

"Shoot the horse," Wolf said again.

"Aw, no, Wolf. Maybe it's not so bad."

Hobart clasped the sore spot with his fingers, gripping the horse's leg just above the ankle. He squeezed, then wrenched the leg as he pressed his ear close to the sore spot. He heard a soft click and Willie lifted its head and let out a horse's shriek.

"Bone's cracked in there, and I think his ankle bone's got a splinter fracture in it," Hobart said. "I had a horse step into a gopher hole and get hurt that same damned way."

He let the hoof fall away from his hand and stood up. He looked at Jessup.

"I can ride you double, Tom," he said.

"Huh? What're you sayin', Hobart?"

"I'm saying you got to put Willie down."

"You mean shoot him?"

"Less'n you want him to suffer more. Wolves and coyotes will tear him to pieces and you'll hear his pitiful screamin' ever' night when you go to bed."

"Christ. Willie's a good horse," Jessup said.

"Not no more he ain't," Hobart said. "When my horse broke its ankle in a gopher hole out in Nebraska, I had to put my rifle barrel against his head and blow his brains out. But my horse was sufferin' and there wasn't no way to fix that broke ankle."

"Draw your pistol, Tom," Wolf said. "Make it quick. That horse of yours is in pain and that's the best thing you can do for him."

"I—I don't know if I can shoot Willie. Jesus."

"Best thing you can do for him now, Tom," Hobart said.

"Get on with it," Wolf said impatiently. "Draw your pistol, or I can use my rifle. One way or another, you got to do it. Ain't no sense in leavin' Willie to suffer like he is."

"Well, God damn it," Jessup said. "It's hard."

"You'll feel better when you put a halt to Willie's sufferin', Tom," Hobart said.

Jessup walked around and jerked his rifle from its scabbard. He levered a cartridge into the firing chamber. The horse sidled a half step away from him as if it knew the end was near.

Jessup began to sob. He sniffled and wept as he walked close to Willie's head and held his rifle up with both hands. He put the snout of the barrel up behind Willie's ear.

"Go ahead," Hobart said. "The longer you wait, the harder it will get."

Jessup let out a loud sob and squeezed the trigger.

The explosion was loud, loud as a thunderclap.

The horse staggered and dropped to his knees. Then he wheezed a last breath and toppled over on his side. His hind legs quivered and kicked three or four times and then he lay still. Jessup's rifle dropped as a tendril of smoke spiraled up from the muzzle.

"Mount up," Wolf ordered both men. "We can't dawdle."

Jessup's head bowed as he looked at Willie's corpse. A shudder went through his body and he wiped tears from his face and snot from his nose with a swipe of his coat sleeve.

"Hate to leave my saddle there," Jessup said as he walked toward Hobart. "And my saddlebags."

"Maybe you can come back on a new horse and fetch 'em in a day or so," Hobart said. He climbed up into the saddle and stretched out a hand to help Jessup climb up behind him using the empty stirrup as a step.

Jessup grasped Hobart's hand and pulled himself up and

swung his leg over the rump of his horse. He scooted up close to the cantle and rested the stock of his rifle on his leg.

"Better wrap an arm around my waist, Tom," Hobart said as he leaned over to retrieve his reins.

Jessup wrapped his right arm halfway around Hobart's waist. "Won't work," he said.

"Grab hold of my belt, then, and hang on," Hobart said.

Jessup lifted Hobart's coat and tucked four fingers inside his gun belt. He gripped the leather tightly as Hobart clucked to his horse and ticked the animal's flanks with his spurs.

As they rode away, Jessup looked back at Willie and stifled a deep sob.

"Good-bye, old boy," Tom murmured and leaned his head against Hobart's back.

"I'll take the lead," Wolf said. He rode around and took up the road in front of Hobart. And now he looked back over his shoulder.

How much time had that lame horse cost them? Was anyone following them?

Wolf didn't know.

"You keep your eyes peeled from now on, Hobart," he said as he looked back at the man riding behind him.

"Sure thing, Wolf," Hobart said. "You can do the same, Tom."

"Is somebody follerin' you?" Jessup asked.

"Likely," Hobart said. "Don't know for sure."

"Jesus," Jessup said. "What a hell of a night."

"You can say that again," Hobart said. But he didn't mean it literally. He was just stiffened up with the cold and wanted the dark night to end.

The road stretched into infinity before them, and there wasn't a lighted lamp anywhere Hobart looked. His back was warm, at least, from Jessup's embrace, but his hands and fingers were still made of cold iron and his arms were riddled with chill bumps.

It was colder than the hinges of hell, he thought, and not yet midnight.

Where in hell, he wondered, was Pagosa Springs?

He kept looking back, but saw nothing and no one.

Ahead, Wolf rode on, glancing every so often upward at the North Star from habit.

Jessup mourned Willie in silence.

Hobart gritted his teeth and kept flexing his fingers inside his gloves.

Wolf thought it was the blackest night he had ever seen, and back in some part of his mind, he knew that they were being followed. He was as sure of it as he was sure of the night and the cold.

Somewhere, behind them, rode the man in black.

Slocum.

A name that made his ire rise every time he thought of it.

He tapped his coat as if to reassure himself that he was still wearing his pistol.

If Slocum was on his trail, he knew he would need it.

Sooner or later.

28

Slocum knew that they were riding through a great gorge formed some 200 million years ago by the massive ice sheet that pushed up the mountains. Sometime during that ice melt, a mighty river had coursed through the Rocky Mountains and carved that gorge where Durango now stood. The only trace was the Animas River.

He also knew that he and Clara faced a sixty-mile ride in darkness to Pagosa Springs. The old wagon road cut through the mountains and into the gorge. He was sure he could find the road because it made a steep drop into the huge canyon. Up on the plain, they would be surrounded by snowcapped peaks that ringed the region. He remembered riding through that huge basin that seemed to have been swept almost clean by ancient glaciers that rumbled across the land, pushing up dirt and rock to form the Rockies, which now stood like silent sentinels over a once-ravaged land that had seen much violence in ancient times.

None of that knowledge gave him much comfort as he and Clara rode into the teeth of the wind that blew from the north, ruffling the river and peppering their faces with grit and a fierce, biting cold.

"It's going to get worse, Clara," he said as they left Durango behind them and plunged into a darkness deepened by the steep walls of towering cliffs on either side of the bumpy uneven road.

162

Clara reached into a pocket of her coat.

"I brought a wool scarf," she said, and flourished it like a banner that blew it almost level along her side.

"Better wrap it on," Slocum said.

He pulled up his bandanna and made a robber's mask over his nose and mouth. It was not enough, but it was better than nothing.

"How far to Pagosa Springs?" she asked as she wrapped her face with the scarf.

"Sixty miles," he said.

"Oh my," she said and bowed her head against the brunt of the wind.

He didn't tell her that it would seem like more miles than that until they rode out of the deep gorge and onto the plain.

It gave him some comfort to know that Wolf and Hobart were probably wishing they were back in Durango, lying in warm beds, their blankets piled on top of them.

He had a high regard for the original white men who had trapped in the mountains during the cold of winter. And now, it was only late summer. The mountain men must have gone through hell to set their traps in freezing waters, build little log huts, and wade through waist-high snow to service their traplines. He had met some of the old-timers who had trapped marten, mink, and beaver, and they were all tough as hickory nuts, and wouldn't have traded their lives for anything. To them, the mountains were sacred, and civilization only a place where they could trade valuable furs for money to buy whiskey, supplies, and maybe the company of a white woman. The mountains were their own special realm where they reigned as kings, a place of magnificent beauty and plentiful game. In the Rockies, they had found sustenance and a peace that could not be matched.

"Stay behind me," he told Clara. "That way, you won't get mashed by so much wind."

"I'll take you up on that," Clara said through chattering teeth.

So they rode single file up the trail with the wind whipping at their coats and burrowing through their boots and socks.

Slocum had to tie his hat down with a leather thong under

his chin. He bowed his head to deflect some of the wind from his face. His forehead had turned into a frozen block of granite, and his fingers, encased in heavy gloves, were fast losing all feeling as the chill slowed the blood in his capillaries and searched under his skin for layers of fat and solid bones.

Above them, Slocum knew, deer and elk were feeding in the stands of timber, roaming through the phalanxes of pine trees, juniper, spruce, and thick brush, protected from the wind, on guard against marauding wolves and the packs of yelping coyotes. But there was no way up those steep cliffs to less hostile ground. They had to make their way through the gorge until they struck the road eastward to Pagosa Springs.

And high above them, too, mountain lions roamed the rimrock, sniffing for prey, bounding gracefully over huge boulders and crags like tawny shadows, silent and almost invisible.

A few miles from town, Slocum heard something.

He halted and held up his hand to stay Clara from advancing any farther.

"What is it?" she asked as she came alongside him and slightly to his rear.

"I heard a rock crack up on the rimrock," he said.

"What?"

"Temperature. When it drops, some of those rocks and boulders get mighty unstable. The cold makes them shrink some, and if they are on soft ground, they can tumble."

"What do you mean?" she asked.

"I've seen avalanches at night in some of these canyons. You don't want to be underneath one if a big boulder loses its footing and comes rumbling down the cliff."

"No, I would think not," she said.

They waited and Slocum listened.

There, he heard it again, the scrape of rock against rock.

He looked up toward the top of the high cliff and beyond, to the stars. The moon was just gliding into view above the tall pines in an inky sky. The stars seemed brighter from the bottom of the gorge, and the Milky Way was a brilliant tapestry of glittering diamonds so far away a man could not even imagine the vast distance.

Then there was a loud scraping sound, a rumble, ahead of them and atop the barren cliff.

"Here it comes," Slocum said. "Duck your head."

Clara looked up in the direction where Slocum pointed with his gloved hand, his arm outstretched.

She did not duck her head as sparks, brilliant and golden, erupted from the top of the cliff. A huge boulder rolled downward, leaving a fiery trail that ignited small bushes in its way. As it gathered speed, it set fire to the larger brush clinging to the cliff face. The boulder roared as it tumbled down the slope like some errant comet with a bright, flaming tail.

"My God, John," Clara exclaimed.

They both watched as the boulder roared down the rest of the cliff face, bounded over the road in a fiery orange and yellow streak, and tumbled into the river. There was a mighty splash and a hissing sound as the boulder abruptly cooled and then split in two as it struck a rock in the streambed.

Slocum waited as the split rock settled and the silence returned.

"What a magnificent sight," Clara said. "Was that an avalanche?"

"No. One big rock loosened up and came down. If it had been an avalanche, the whole top of the mountain might have come down on us."

"Oh, my. Is it safe to go on?"

"I think so. Just keep your eyes open, if you can in this stiff wind, and I'll listen. Some pebbles could come down after that rock let loose, but they shouldn't harm us."

"Are you sure?" she asked apprehensively.

"Don't worry," he said and laughed.

They both heard a rattling above and ahead of them, as loosened gravel slid downward. But none loosened any more rocks and none reached the road.

They rode past the place where the boulder had put on such a fireworks display, and there were no more such incidents.

There was only the wind, and it chilled them both to the bone.

Clara was not so exposed as Slocum, but she could feel it.

She was cold and miserable. She thought of warm places and warm times, and that helped her to deal with the cold. She looked at the back of the tall man and was glad he was right in front of her on his black horse. She trusted him and she had never trusted any man until then.

The years seemed to drop away from her as she gazed at Slocum's strong and sturdy back. Had she met him years ago, she might never have had to endure the humiliation and pain of those lonely, dreary years with Wolf Steiner.

But, she reasoned, the past could not be erased. They had not met and each had lived separate lives. Now Fate had drawn them together and there was a fullness in her heart that she had not experienced since she had been a child. She felt rich beyond measure to have made a friend in John Slocum. And finally fulfilled, since they had coupled together on his bed. She could still feel him inside her, still feel that swollen member plumbing deep into her womb, and she could recall the thrill of her many climaxes and the beauty of lovemaking that had made her feel, finally, like a real woman, a woman loved.

Slocum saw the cut in the road just ahead and breathed a half sigh of relief. He worked his fingers inside his gloves, hoping to restore feeling from the blood flow. He wriggled his toes inside his boots, glad that he had worn heavy woolen socks instead of the cotton ones he carried with him.

"There's the road to Pagosa Springs," he said as he turned to look at Clara.

"Mmmm," she mumbled. She shook all over from the cold and could not even form words from her frozen lips.

They turned up the road, and the wind subsided considerably. It was a long steep climb to the basin above them, but at least they were out of the bruising wind that they had faced head-on.

They rode for another hour after they had topped the crown of the road and made their way across a vast plain where mountains glowed in the distance with their snowcapped peaks.

A while later, Slocum slowed Ferro and approached an object at the side of the road. Long before he reached it, he knew what it was. He beckoned for Clara to ride up alongside him.

"Looks like a dead horse up ahead," he said.

"I see something," she said.

The wind still blew across the plain, but it was warmer and not as brisk.

Slocum slowed to a stop as they reached the horse. He looked down at it, and even in the dark, with the moon high above them, he could see the bullet hole in the horse's brain.

"Why, I know that horse," Clara said.

"You do?"

"Yes. His name is Willie, and he belongs, belonged, to one of Wolf's men. Yes, that's Tom's horse. Tom Jessup. I wonder what happened."

"Probably went lame on him," Slocum said. "I noticed a hole back there in the road. I rode around it."

"I never saw it."

"But you followed me. Bad thing for a horse to go lame out here. Hold on a minute. I'm going to take a closer look."

Clara shivered and clasped her arms around her as if that would help to warm her. It did not, but the illusion was there.

Slocum dismounted and with numb fingers dug out a box of lucifers. He shielded the match against the north wind and struck it as he bent over.

The match flared, and he examined the ground all around the horse. He saw boot prints and the hoof marks of two horses.

Easy to figure, he thought.

Wolf and Hobart had stopped here. The man named Tom Jessup had probably been reluctant to shoot his horse and Wolf had talked him into it.

The match went out and Slocum struck another one.

He walked back and forth, staring at the horse tracks.

One of the horses had taken on extra weight. Its hooves had dug deeper into the ground.

"Likely, your Tom is riding double. That'll slow Wolf some. But none of us are going to gallop across this piece of prairie anyway."

"No. Not in this wind," Clara said.

Slocum let the match die out and dropped its skeleton onto the ground. He climbed back up in the saddle.

"How far ahead do you think Wolf and Hobart are?" she asked.

"Wind's blowing sand and dust into those tracks. Two hours ahead maybe. Way more than an hour. Hard to read such tracks in the dark."

"You're a good tracker," she said.

"Fair," he replied and spurred Ferro to set out along the road.

"We won't catch them tonight, will we?" she asked as she rode alongside Slocum.

"Not likely. Not unless they stop or make camp. And that's not likely either."

"No, I supposed it's not," she said. "Oh, John, I'm so glad I'm with you."

"You're crazy," he said. "You could be home in bed, warm and safe."

"I'd rather be with you," she said, and immediately wished she had not spoken those words. Slocum might get the idea that she was chasing him. "I meant . . ." she started to say.

"I know what you mean," he said. "You want Wolf dead as much as I do."

"Yes, yes, I do, John."

"Be patient," he said. "And stay sharp."

"I will," she said.

They rode on and the wind dropped. It was still very chilly, but Slocum began to get feeling back in his fingers and toes.

Slocum could not gauge the miles they had come, or the miles they had yet to go. But he knew he was on the right track. Somewhere ahead, three men rode and they were all headed for Pagosa Springs.

Distance was difficult to measure. He could see the shining white tops of the mountain range in the distance, but in the high mountain air, mountains always appeared closer than they actually were.

He looked over at Clara alongside him. She was a tough one, he thought. She would have made some man a good wife. She was made of solid pioneer stock, like the women who had come west with their men in covered wagons to settle and build homes, bear and raise children, grow food while their husbands hunted wild game. He had great admiration for such women, and when he looked at Clara's strong face, he knew she belonged in their company.

At another time and place, perhaps, he and Clara might have married and both lived different lives.

But he was what he was, and she was what she was.

There was no changing who they were, he knew.

For now, though, they were riding together and they both had the same wish. It was enough to form a bond between them in this time and place.

And he was glad that she was with him, and he with her.

That was enough, too.

29

Miriam Hellinger opened the firebox on the iron cookstove and dropped two sticks of kindling into it. Her kitchen was filled with a pleasant steam, the delicious aroma of Arbuckle's coffee with its cinnamon stick wafting through the small house as it had for the two years she and Abner had been in Durango. She clapped the lid back on the firebox and moved the coffee-pot off the hot lid to a space in between and the burbling lessened as the coffee cooled.

Abner sat at the table in the dining room, his suspenders loosened, his bare feet in a warm bowl of water. He had not done so much walking since he was a kid going to school every day, four and a half miles from his house in Illinois.

Miriam had found a box of old flyers he had inherited when he took the job of constable and brought it down for him to look through.

"I knowed I heard that name somewhere," she called from the kitchen as she set out two heavy tin cups on a beer tray she had bought in New Mexico some years before.

"What name is that?" Abner asked as he set papers in a pile.

"John Slocum. But I didn't hear it. I saw it when you took this blamed job as constable and toted all them wanted dodgers home from your office."

"You got a good memory, Miriam," he said. "Seems like I recollect seein' his name somewhere, too."

"I was rummaging up in the loft today while you was out gallivantin' around town and danged if I didn't see it in that wooden box. Should be on top, all yellered and stained, smellin' of mold and such. Bunch of spiders in that box, but I mashed all their eggs and they run off."

She poured coffee into the two cups and carried the tray to the table where Abner sat.

"I found it," he said. "Right on top. But I'm just lookin' at some of the others. Amazin' how many outlaws are on the run with prices on their heads."

"And you never caught a one of 'em," she said, a malicious grin on her chubby face. She sat down and lifted Abner's cup from the tray.

She had gained weight the past two years. She tried to hide the folds of fat on her body with flouncy dresses and an apron, but she couldn't deny that she had gotten fat. Only she didn't use that term. Ever. The word she used was "stout."

"I'm a mite stout," she would say when the other women in town chided her about the weight gain.

But Abner liked her that way. Or said he did.

"More of you to love," he would say when she wallowed in bed at night with his hands roaming over her plump breasts and flabby belly. "I like a woman with some meat on her."

He always made her laugh when he said that, and she always vowed she'd eat fewer potatoes and pork fat and stop buying candy at the store.

"Why don't you set that box down, Abner, and drink your coffee? You found what you was lookin' for. That John Slocum you keep talkin' about is wanted in Georgia for killin' a judge. There's a bounty on his head we could use. Five hunnert dollars."

Abner put the pile of flyers back in the wooden box and set it on the floor. He wriggled his feet in the warm water with the Epsom salts soothing his tired feet.

He picked up his coffee cup in one hand, the wanted sheet in the other. He blew steam off his cup and sipped.

"Yep, that's the man," he said. "Younger when this picture was drawed. And his hair was shorter, too. But it's definitely him."

"We could use the reward money, Abner," she said. She took a sip from her cup and it burned her tongue.

"This is an old dodger," he said. "And he wasn't tried and convicted for no murder back in Calhoun County, Georgia. Just says he's wanted as a suspect in a judge's murder."

"So what difference does that make?" she asked.

"Law says a man is innocent until proved guilty."

"Oh, pshaw, Abner, the man is wanted by the law and you ought to collect that reward."

He looked at Miriam as he set the flyer aside and picked up his cup. He sloshed his feet gently in the warm water and salts. Soothing.

"Georgia's a fur piece. I'd have to haul him back there to collect the reward."

"Or turn him over to the U.S. marshal," she said.

"And wait for the money. Maybe years."

Abner shook his head and drank more coffee. He could taste the cinnamon, and the coffee was strong.

He and Craig had arrested two more of Wolf's men after putting Loomis in jail. Billy Joe Vernon and Gabe Tolliver. Caught them red-handed at Wilbur Nichols's cabin, prying open the dead man's strongbox and filling up a sack with Wilbur's possessions. Common thieves, but part of Wolf's claim-jumping gang. He and Craig had walked in with guns drawn and put the handcuffs on them after pulling their pistols from their holsters. One of them, Billy Joe, had a knot on his head from when Craig thunked him with the butt of his pistol. Abner had added resisting arrest to the charges of robbery and accomplice to murder.

Now he had three men stewing in his small jail and his feet were swollen from walking on gravel and rocks.

And from all accounts, Slocum was chasing after Wolf Steiner and the rest of his bunch. A man like that was worth more than five hundred dollars, he thought.

"Well, Miriam, the wheels of justice move slow," he said as he leaned back in his chair, sniffing the scent of the Arbuckle's.

"What's that mean, Abner?" she asked. Her small mouth was even smaller with the round plumpness of her oval face. Her nose smaller, too. Her hazel eyes sparkled in the lamplight with yellows and greens and a spot or two of russet.

"It means that Slocum has done this town a service."

"A service? What service?"

"He uncovered a murderous gang of claim jumpers, for one thing. He shot the men who killed poor Jasper Nichols, a boy who never hurt a flea. He's got Wolf Steiner on the run, along with maybe a couple more of them cutthroat backshooters."

"That's justice?" Miriam asked as she raised her cup once again to her tiny little lips.

"Frontier justice, maybe."

"I don't know what that is, Abner. Frontier justice. Pshaw."

"It means when the law is slack, a man who gives a damn can be the law hisself."

"Well, I never heard of such a thing," she said with a huff of breath.

"Slocum didn't have to do what he did. He brought some horses here for Lou Darvin. His business was finished. But he saw a man get blowed out of his mine and he took it on hisself to see that Wilbur and Jasper Nichols got some justice. And he probably saved Lou's life to boot."

"That makes him a lawman?"

"No, I'm not sayin' that. But it puts him on the side of the law, and that's worth something. I'm just one man here and I got a deputy who don't have the brains of a pissant, and we're supposed to keep the peace in a town that's just one hair away from lawlessness. When you got gold in the ground, you got greed. And greed makes some men cross over the line and take up the criminal life."

"Maybe you ought to have a little greed for yourself, Abner," she said as her coffee cooled and she could drink it without blowing on it.

"Greed is an ugly thing, Miriam. I want no part of it. You shouldn't either."

"I just want what I have comin' to me," she said with a trace of defiance in her voice. "That's all."

"Where do you draw the line?" Abner asked.

Miriam gave him a blank look.

He looked at her and thought about Slocum. The man might have a price on his head, but he was no common criminal. Maybe he killed a judge in Georgia, and maybe he didn't. It wasn't the constable's job to be judge, jury, and executioner. Hellinger had Durango to take care of, and that was enough for him.

"What're you going to do, Abner?" she asked as he set his cup down and stood up.

"I've got one more man to shackle," he said. "A crook who deserves time in jail. I'm going to serve him with a search warrant in the morning and haul him off to the hoosegow."

"Who?" she asked.

"Abel Fogarty. He's as crooked as a snake and we don't need his kind in this town."

"Is Elmer goin' with you?"

"Yep. First thing in the morning."

"What about Slocum? What are you going to do about him and the reward?"

"Ah, Slocum. I'm going to do nothin'. If he comes back with Wolf and the rest of his gang, I'll shake his hand and maybe pat him on the back."

"And then, just let him go?"

"Yep. Just let him go, Miriam. That's the right thing to do."

"Abner, you're a fool. A damned ignorant fool."

"I'm going to get some shut-eye, Miriam. You can use that flyer there on the table to light your breakfast fire in the morning. I'm goin' to bed."

He sopped across the floor with bare wet feet and walked to their bedroom. He was tired and there was so much to do early in the morning.

"Good night, Abner," Miriam called as he left the hallway.

"Good night, Miriam."

He hoped he would see Slocum again. There was something about the man that he admired. No matter what his past was, Slocum was a man to ride the river with and didn't deserve to rot away in some Georgia prison.

That's what Abner would call justice, not the label society put on a man. Slocum was a free man and he deserved to stay that way.

One thing was for sure, Abner vowed.

Slocum would never spend a minute in the Durango jail.

30

The night wore on, weary mile by weary mile. And although the moon was up, and the road easier, Wolf, Hobart, and Jessup were displaying signs of extreme fatigue. And so were the two horses, one of them packing double.

"I'm plumb tuckered out, Wolf," Hobart said sometime toward morning. "Horse is about played out, too."

"We got three and a half more days of hard riding ahead of us, Hobart. Quit your damned bellyachin'."

Wolf had his own weariness to deal with and resented Hobart's complaint. To him, that was a sign of weakness.

And he was still looking over his shoulder. More often, now that they were in the open, than before. His and Hobart's horses were sturdy enough, but the hard ride through the gorge had sapped their strength. So, too, had the climb out of the deep canyon onto higher ground.

Where was Slocum? he wondered.

So far, he had seen no sign that anyone was pursuing them. But they were long days from Pagosa Springs, and the horses did show signs that they needed rest. His own muscles were still kinked up from the cold, and while it was a sight warmer up on the plain, it was still cold as all get-out.

Besides looking over his back trail, Wolf had his eye to the north as well. That darkness in the gorge wasn't all night; there were ugly black clouds looming beyond the glow of the moon.

They were not close, but they had the wind at their backs and he dreaded that they might bring a hell of a rainstorm in the morning. Rain and thunder and lightning. That would hinder them even more, slow them down. They might even have to seek shelter or crawl under their horses' bellies to stay reasonably dry.

He was full of unvoiced curses. But he was not going to give Hobart or Jessup the satisfaction of knowing that he was as tired as they were.

"We shoulda gone into the timber and rested up before heading for the Springs," Hobart said.

"That climb up the mountain would have set us back a good two more days," Wolf said.

"Yeah, but we could've built us a lean-to and stayed out of the wind."

"Go on back if you want," Wolf said. "Maybe you want a sugar tit to suck on, too."

"Aw, Wolf. I was just ruminatin'."

"Well, ruminate all you want. We're going on, come hell or high water, and if you don't like it, you can turn back and maybe dangle at the end of a rope."

"Shit, Wolf. Ain't you got no heart? My horse is packin' double and about to cave in. And I'm so tired, my eyes are jumpin' with bugs what ain't there."

"Close them, then. The horse knows the way."

"Yeah, but my horse is about to lose what legs he's got left."

"What do you want to do? Stop and let Slocum catch up with us? You want a shoot-out with that trigger-happy bastard? We got to go on, Hobart. Ain't no gettin' around it."

"Yeah, I know. I was just makin' a comment. Not that it did any good."

"Gripin' don't pay the toll," Wolf said. "And grumblin' don't pay the rent."

Hobart clamped his mouth shut.

But Jessup spoke up. Not to Wolf, but to Hobart.

"Hobart?"

"Yeah?"

Their voices were deliberately low so that Wolf wouldn't hear them.

"I'm tired, too. Can't hardly hold on no more," Jessup said.

"Hell, all you got to do is sit. I got to wrassle this horse so's he don't fall asleep on his feet."

"I know. I just wish we could stop, maybe rest some and stretch our legs. I got no feelin' in mine."

"Well, Wolf says we go on. So we go on. Maybe he'll stop by and by. Less'n he's made of iron."

"I wish my horse hadn't gone lame," Jessup said.

"Well, he did, and now you got no horse, Tom. Move your legs up and down. Maybe that'll start the blood to flowin' and you'll get some feelin' back."

Jessup tried that, first with one leg, then the other. He almost fell off. But he held tight to the back of Hobart's gun belt. His legs were beyond numbness. They felt like they had turned to rock. He tried it again and realized that his butt was without feeling as well. It had gone as numb as his legs.

And the wind picked up again. The dark clouds to the north looked more ominous. Closer.

Wolf pumped up and down in the saddle, restoring feeling to his legs and feet. His horse started to stumble and he jerked the reins hard, sliding the bit into the tender part of his mouth. The horse tossed his head and whinnied in protest.

He stretched his arms, one by one, and flexed his fingers.

There was no way to keep the wind from filtering in through the eyeholes in his shirt where it was buttoned, or the seam in front. His neck was chilled, and the shirt was rubbing against it, irritating the skin.

Wolf knew he was pushing it. Perhaps Hobart was right. They should have taken to the timber, where they could have built a shelter out of spruce boughs, held the wind at bay, and gotten some rest. But to turn back now would be sheer suicide.

He knew damned well that Slocum was on his trail. He was somewhere behind them. Maybe he shouldn't have killed that gal, Amy. But he had wanted revenge for her getting Jimmy John sliced up like mincemeat. The treacherous bitch. Her and Slocum. Two of a kind, and a thorn, a big sharp thorn, in his side.

In a way, he hoped that he and Slocum would come

face-to-face. He would like nothing better than to blow that bastard's brains out. The thought was both delicious and comforting as he rode on, his horse stumbling every so often, every bone in his body aching.

Get it over and done with.

After all, Slocum was the only thing stopping him from doing what he wanted to do in Durango. With enough mining claims, he could take Clara and Stacey way out West where nobody knew them, maybe buy a little ranch and raise some cattle.

He seldom thought about Clara, but she sprang into his mind. She was his only connection to his past, to his twin brother. And she was a constant reminder of how treacherous women were. She picked the wrong man to marry, and he had made her pay for it, the bitch.

His thoughts were all over the place now, and he wondered if those spots dancing before his eyes were a sign that he needed sleep, or that he was no longer in control of his senses. He still looked back over his shoulder, but the land swam and there could have been an army on his back trail for all he knew.

They crossed a small creek and let the horses drink.

"Maybe we ought to bide here awhile," Hobart said. "Give the horses a handful of grain."

"We ain't stoppin'," Wolf said. "Now get that idea out of your sorry head, Hobart."

The horses drank and they rode on, much slower than before.

"I'm hungry," Tom Jessup whined. He spoke so low that Wolf did not hear him, but Hobart did.

"Dig into my saddlebag, the left one," Hobart said. "There's some beef jerky wrapped in butcher paper and maybe an old biscuit or two."

"Thanks, Hobart," Tom said, and he opened the flap on Hobart's saddlebag, felt around with chilled, ungainly fingers until something rattled inside the bag.

He pulled out the butcher paper rolled up around strips of jerky that felt stiff but moldy in the soft spots.

He pulled one out and chewed on it. It tasted like dried horseshit, but he didn't say anything to Hobart.

One piece was enough for Tom. He rerolled the paper and

put the packet back in Hobart's saddlebag. His stomach churned and he thought he might not be able to keep the food down.

He looked over at Wolf. The man was a monster, he thought.

Wolf sat straight in his saddle, rising up on his stirrups every so often and looking over his shoulder.

Jessup wondered now why he had ever gotten hooked up with a man like Wolf Steiner. He knew the answer. Money. A chance for more money than he had ever seen in his life.

Wolf tried to spur his horse to pick up more speed, but the animal balked and did not break into a faster gait. He cursed under his breath and he knew he would gain no ground this day on Slocum.

When he stood up in his stirrups again and gazed back down the long plain, he thought he saw a dark shape on the very tip of the horizon. He rubbed one of his eyes and looked again.

The plain was empty.

But for a long time after that, he could not shake the feeling that he had seen a man on horseback. A darker blob than the night darkness.

Could he really see that far in the dark?

He shook his head and decided that it was not possible. His eyes were playing tricks on him.

But deep down, he knew Slocum was on his trail. He was coming.

And in his present state of mind and physical condition, Wolf wondered if he could ward off such a powerful and deadly adversary.

Only time would tell.

31

The nearly full moon cast a pale light over the plain. Every bush, every rock bore a pewter cast, and the road was a ghostly ribbon that stretched into infinity.

Slocum called a halt when he gauged that they had covered nearly ten miles of the sixty-mile ride to Pagosa Springs. He figured that they should be able to make between twelve and fifteen miles a day, but it could very well take them longer since, when the grain ran out, they'd have to let their horses graze, and they'd also have to stop for water at the creeks and springs along the way.

He knew that Clara had to be tired.

Yet so far, she had not complained. The horses seemed to be doing fine now that they were out of the strong winds that had besieged them in the narrow gorge.

Now he saw the building clouds far to the north, clouds that were eating up stars as they blew their way on the heels of the wind that had tormented them when they were down in the gorge.

"Want to stop and rest the horses?" Slocum asked after an hour's riding across the plain.

"I see no reason to stop just yet, John," she said. She patted her horse's neck. "Horse seems fine. She's not shivering anymore."

"Are you?" he asked as they rode along.

"Nope. I'm not warm, but I don't have the chilblains no more."

"You let me know, Clara. We're going to stop anyway in another hour or two, to give our horses some of that grain."

"That'll be fine," she said.

He wondered. Clara was tough, but she also had the man who was responsible for the murder of her daughter on her mind. Not to mention the same man who had murdered her husband and abused her for twenty miserable years.

Clara had grit, he decided. And plenty of it.

He had no idea how far ahead Wolf, Hobart, and Jessup were, but they were packing double on one horse and they had left Durango at a full gallop. Their horses were made of sturdy stock, but they would need water and feed. They would also need rest.

He had the feeling that, despite their slow pace, they might be gaining on Wolf. Slowly maybe, a yard or two at a time, but steadily, like the tortoise chasing after the hare.

Another two hours passed. Then Slocum called a halt as he caught a glimpse of something odd on the ground.

"Why are we stopping?" Clara asked.

"I want to light a lucifer and take a look at those tracks," he said. "You stay put. Catch your breath."

"I will," she said.

Slocum stepped down out of the saddle and removed a box of matches from his pocket. He struck one as he squatted down and waved it slowly over the horse tracks of the men he was pursuing. He waddled a ways, with the match still lit, cupped by his hand to shield it from the north wind.

Then he let the match go out and stood up. He walked over to where Clara sat her horse.

"What did you find?" she asked.

"One of the horses is dragging one foot every so often. The other is plowing ground up with its hooves."

"What does that tell you, John?" she asked.

"It tells me that their horses are tiring. Tiring fast."

"And so?"

"So unless they want their horses to founder in another ten or twenty miles, Wolf is going to have to stop and give those horses a rest."

"He won't stop," she said.

"He's not that stupid, is he?" Slocum looked up at her face, which was still bundled with her scarf up to her nostrils.

"He doesn't care about horses or people. He'd ride a horse to death if it would get him where he wanted to go." Her words were muffled through the scarf, but Slocum understood every word.

"He'd have a good forty miles on foot if he does that," Slocum said. "That would be stupid."

"Well, he might stop. He's not stupid, John. Wolf is a very clever man. Cruel, but clever."

"So many of them are," he said. "I've known clever men who could have made a living legitimately, but some twist in their thinking, or in their brains, makes them turn to crime."

"Like Wolf," she said.

"Yeah, like Wolf. Exactly."

He mounted Ferro and clucked to him. He did not have to touch his blunted spurs to his flanks. Ferro stepped out like the obedient steed he was, and they rode on, still at that slow, relentless pace.

They stopped at the same creek where Wolf had watered their horses. Both he and Clara walked around to restore circulation in their cold legs while the two horses snuffled and slobbered in the stream, drinking the water slow, seeming to enjoy the brief respite. When they were halfway through drinking, Slocum poured oats and corn into the crown of his hat and fed each one.

Then the horses drank again.

"You didn't give them much grain," Clara said as they both remounted their horses.

"Just enough fuel to get them a few more miles. If we don't catch up with Wolf by dawn, we'll have to make camp. Give the horses and ourselves a rest."

"Will you cuddle me?" she said. "In your bedroll."

"We could exchange some warmth, yes," he said with a wicked smile.

"I could use some sleep," she said as she rubbed her eyes.

"And some cuddling?"

"Yes, just what a woman needs."

"Don't leave out the man. Men need cuddling every once in a while, too."

"I had no idea," she said.

"Like hell you didn't, Clara. If ever there was a woman who knew what a man needed, it's you."

"Why, that's very nice of you to say, John. I'm pleased. You make me feel like a real woman."

"You are a real woman," he said.

The sky lightened and the eastern horizon changed into a mother-of-pearl glow, spreading a pale light over the rocky, bush-dotted plain. The mountaintops glistened a brilliant white as if they had been freshly painted, or scrubbed. The air was invigorating despite the increased intensity of the wind.

To the north, Slocum saw the bulging elephantine clouds, black as the inside of a deep underground cave. In the distance, they both heard the bass tympanic notes of thunder that rumbled clear to the mountains.

"Storm's coming soon," Slocum said. "You got a slicker in your saddlebags?"

"I sure do," she said.

"Better break it out. From the sound of that thunder, I'd say we have less than a half hour before we're hit by a wall of rain."

She reached back and opened one of her saddlebags. She withdrew a blue slicker that was wadded up into a tight ball. She shook it out and her mare shied and sidestepped at the unexpected sight and sound.

Slocum removed a black slicker from his saddlebag and slipped it on as they rode on into the pale glow of the eastern sky.

He stood up in his stirrups to gaze far ahead of them. Where the road disappeared, he saw something yellow. He judged the distance to be a little more than two miles.

He eased himself back into the saddle and looked over at Clara, who was buttoning her raincoat.

"They're not far ahead of us," he said.

She turned swiftly to look at him.

"What?"

"I see a flash of yellow slickers up ahead. Just on the rim of the horizon. That's Wolf and his boys. Has to be."

She felt her pulse quicken. "Are you sure?"

"Unless the prairie is blossoming in great big yellow leaves, yes."

She stood up in her stirrups. She caught just a glimpse of

the yellow slickers and then they disappeared over the horizon.

"I saw them," she said. "At least I saw something."

"Steady. That storm's going to hit us before we catch up to them."

He looked down at the ground. The horse tracks showed him that both horses were scuffing the ground with the front of their hooves. They were tired and not making much speed. Usually, the hoofprints would have been distinct, but these were moiled and left clumps of dirt and scrapes where they dragged the ground.

Ten minutes later, they saw jagged streaks of lightning, and thunder boomed with concussive effect. The wind picked up, and then the rain suddenly drenched them in a glimmering sheet. Tails sprouted beneath the black clouds, and there was a dimming of the light as the clouds began to block the rising sun.

"What do we do now?" Clara asked above the roar of thunder.

"Catch up to them," Slocum said.

She huddled down when the rain hit. In moments they were drenched.

"Let's see what our horses can do," he said, and touched spurs to Ferro's flanks. The horse stepped out in a desultory trot. Clara followed him on her Rose.

They gained ground on Wolf. When they had gone a mile, they saw the yellow slickers ahead of them, less than half a mile away.

"There they are," Clara said, pointing a rain-soaked glove at the trio on horseback.

"Time for a showdown," Slocum said, and slowed Ferro to a walk.

The riders ahead seemed like blind men groping for a way out of an unfamiliar room.

The rain sounded loud on their slickers. Lightning flashed in crooked staircases within the low black clouds. Thunder roared in their ears and seemed to shake the ground.

They came within a hundred yards of Wolf, Hobart, and Jessup.

Slocum drew his rifle from its scabbard and levered a cartridge into the chamber. He rested the barrel across the arch of his pommel, next to his saddle horn.

The riders ahead of them stopped. They turned their horses and waited.

The heavy rain drowned out most of the sound.

Slocum saw the man on the lone horse raise his hands to his mouth.

"That you, Slocum?" Wolf shouted above the sound of the hammering rain.

Slocum held one hand to his mouth and drew in on Ferro's reins.

"It's me, Wolf. Your time is up."

"Like hell it is, you sonofabitch."

Clara snaked her rifle from its sheath. She levered a cartridge out of the magazine and into the firing chamber.

"Who you got with you, Slocum?" Wolf called.

Slocum said nothing, but looked at Clara.

"It's me, you bastard—Clara," she shouted.

Wolf roared with sarcastic laughter.

"You got a little old gal to help you, Slocum? You must wear panties, too."

Slocum eased Ferro into a slow walk with a touch of his spurs and a squeeze from both knees. The horse moved like a black wraith toward the three men.

Jessup climbed down from Hobart's horse and started to run down the road, slicker flapping in the wind behind him.

"Slap leather, Wolf, or throw up your hands," Slocum ordered. He slid the barrel of his rifle from the pommel and pointed the muzzle downward.

"You're damned right, Slocum. You're at the end of your damned road." Hobart twisted in his saddle as he drew his pistol.

Wolf drew his own weapon from the holster snugged to his right leg.

Slocum put the rifle to his shoulder and aimed it at Hobart, who was cocking his pistol as he raised it to his eye level.

Slocum aligned the rear buckhorn sight with the front blade sight, and when it settled on Hobart's heart, he squeezed the trigger.

The rifle blared a roaring thunder of its own and the stock bucked against Slocum's shoulder. Smoke poured from the muzzle in a shower of bright red and orange sparks. The smoke evaporated into the pouring rain.

Hobart buckled in his saddle and slumped forward.

Wolf fired his pistol at Slocum.

Slocum heard the sizzle of the bullet as it creased the air a few inches from his left ear. He levered another cartridge into the chamber.

His sights found Wolf's chest and he lowered them slightly before he took in a breath, held it, and gently squeezed the trigger.

Wolf's pistol fell out of his hand to the ground, splashed in a rainy puddle alongside him. His horse reared up and whinnied.

Wolf slid from his saddle and hit the ground with a splash.

"You got him, John!" Clara cried. "You got that bastard."

Slocum rearmed his rifle and rode toward Wolf. The man floundered on the soggy ground, tried to rise.

Wolf was still alive.

He groped for his sodden pistol, fingers flexing like the claws of a crab. He touched the butt and his fingers slid off.

Slocum rode up and stood over Wolf's floundering hulk.

Wolf looked up at him, his gun hand still a few inches away from his weapon.

"I wanted to see you hang, Wolf, but this is good enough. You'll die soon. I give you less than five minutes."

"Fuck you, Slocum," Wolf spat as blood poured from the hole just below his chest. Gushed. Spurted. There was lots of it. He coughed and tried to rise.

Clara rode up and looked down at her tormentor.

"I hope you burn in hell, Wolf," she shouted down at him. "Forever and ever."

"You bitch," Wolf spat and there was blood on his words and in the spittle that dripped over his lips and down his chin. He coughed and struggled for air as blood got sucked into his windpipe. He opened his mouth to say something, but nothing came out except a final rattle in his throat.

"Is he dead?" Clara asked.

"As a doornail," Slocum said.

"Good riddance," she said. Then she spat on Wolf, but the rain left no trace of her spittle.

Hobart was dead, too, his heart splintered and mashed into a bloody pulp. He gazed at nothingness as rain splashed on his open eyes.

Slocum gathered the reins of the two horses and rode a few yards as Clara continued to look down at Wolf's dead body.

"Are you ready to leave?" he called.

"In a minute," she said.

"I'm not going back to Durango, Clara," he said when she rode up close. He'd rescued this damsel in distress, and now she was free to make a new life for herself and her daughter. It was time for him to say good-bye.

"What?"

"I'm sorry, but I've got to go. Business. New territory." He also needed to put some distance between himself and the bitter memories of watching Lacey die and finally losing Amy. Four women—the four damsels of Durango—had been a brief part of his life, but now it was time to ride on.

"I was hoping you'd—"

"I've done what I had to do. You're a fine woman, but here is where we go our separate ways."

He leaned over and kissed her on the lips.

"John . . ."

He turned his head for a minute, then back again.

"You're better off without me, Clara," he said. "Go home and take care of your daughter. She needs you now more than ever. Maybe we'll meet again. At a better time and place."

"You're breaking my heart," she said.

He lifted a hand to wave good-bye.

"No, I think your heart's on the mend. I'm going on to Pagosa Springs. I'll catch up to Tom Jessup and offer him one of these horses."

"You're not going to kill him?"

"There's been enough of that. And I don't think he was involved in any of Wolf's schemes. So long."

Then he turned Ferro and rode off into the rain, leading the two horses.

Behind him, he thought he could hear Clara sobbing, but perhaps it was only the patter of rain on his hat brim.

And the thunder rolled.

Watch for

SLOCUM AND THE BEAST OF FALL PASS

420th novel in the exciting SLOCUM series
from Jove

Coming in February!